PHORESIS

PHORESIS

GREG EGAN

SUBTERRANEAN PRESS 2018

First Edition

ISBN
978-1-59606-866-7

Subterranean Press
PO Box 190106
Burton, MI 48519

subterraneanpress.com

Manufactured in the United States of America

PART ONE

1 ~~~~~

FREYA walked slowly across the ice, using her rake to scrape aside the thin cover of dirt and crystalline powder, peering down into the translucent slab below for any sign of a slender rootlet struggling to force its way out into the air.

Something dark and linear caught her eye, about a hand's breadth deep. She stopped walking and squatted down for a closer look, then she took her pick and swung it into the ice. Once the surface shattered it was impossible to see anything beneath it, but after a dozen blows she stopped and cleared the debris out of the hole she'd made. She'd exposed the inclusion, but it wasn't a root: it was just a streak of trapped gravel.

The sun was behind a bank of reddish clouds that covered most of the western sky and left the ice field in a state of ambiguous gloom, so she glanced up at Tvíburi, hoping to find that the time had sped by while she worked. But the twin world was still just a crescent: the afternoon shift was barely half over.

Freya was tired and hungry. She took a deep breath and held it in to make the most of it; by the time she exhaled she felt a little steadier. The air was thin from the sun's recent tantrums, but thousands of villages besides her own would be performing the same time-tested remedy. The Yggdrasils thrived on the temperature difference between the buried ocean and the cool of the surface, but sometimes their roots didn't make it all the way through the ice. Chipping away the final barrier let them complete their journey—and once they were exposed to the open air, they were free to dispense all the volatile treasures they'd pumped up from below.

Off to her right, her nearest neighbor was intent on her own patch, and too far away to converse with unless they shouted. Freya stopped procrastinating and recommitted herself to the task. The sooner they'd reached their quota, the sooner they could all go home.

∞

THE COMMUNAL TENT was noisy, and the long table was more crowded with diners than food, but Freya was glad to be out of the cold, walking barefoot on the tent's tattered rugs. She eyed the remaining provisions and estimated a fair share, then she gathered the food up quickly before someone assumed she'd lost her appetite.

It was only as she sat down to eat that she realized she'd arrived in the middle of an argument. "And what about the soil?" Gro demanded. "This is just a stopgap! It might help us breathe, but it's not going to give us so much as a handful of new soil."

"You want to dig a whole new geyser while we're out here?"

Hanna teased her. "Cleave through a few thousand strides of ice and…" She gestured with her hands, miming an eruption. "What could be simpler?"

"So if we don't know how to fix the problem, no one should talk about it?" Gro retorted. "In my mother's day, the yields were at least a third more than they are now!"

"So tighten your stomach," Bridget advised.

"And keep your brothers in check," Hanna joked.

Gro's demeanor was becoming increasingly sour. "Will you laugh when your children are born too small and sickly to survive?"

"You didn't tell us you were pregnant," Erna interjected solemnly, tentatively offering Gro some of her own food.

"I'm not!" Gro gripped the table in frustration. "So does anyone else believe that there's a problem? Or am I just imagining it?"

Freya said, "The yields are going down, everyone's seeing it."

"At last! Thank you!" Gro stood up, as if to walk over and embrace her in gratitude, but then she changed her mind and sat down again.

"But I don't know what we can do, except hope for a fresh geyser," Freya added. She had never heard of any kind of intervention that could achieve such a goal.

Gro said, "How about acknowledging that this isn't going to fix itself, and turning our minds to finding a solution?"

There was a moment of silence from the other members of the group, and then Hanna conceded, "There must have been a time before anyone thought about exposing the roots. When they all just sat around, too tired to move, waiting for the air to replenish itself."

"Exactly," Gro replied. "And if they'd kept on that way, we might not even be here now."

"But a *geyser?*" Bridget protested.

"If it were easy," Gro said, "it would have happened long ago. Keep it in your minds, that's all I'm asking. Search your thoughts while you search the ground. It might even help you pass the time."

∞

THE NEXT MORNING, Freya took Gro's advice, staring into the ice as diligently as ever as she trudged across the unbroken plain, but letting the impossible problem sit like a nagging onlooker in the back of her skull.

Geysers came and went, with no apparent pattern to their arrival: bursting out of the ice and then flowing twice a day, lasting anything from a year to a century. As fickle as the sun's own eruptions, they provided an erratic counterbalance to those air-ablating blasts. But while Freya had no idea what caused the solar flares, every child was taught the origin of the geysers.

As Tvíbura and Tvíburi turned together, their mutual orbit swung them around in a single day, compared to the fifteen days it took them to circle the sun. So Tvíbura's choice to fix her gaze upon her twin precluded the same relationship with her light-giving mother—and just as well, on every count Freya could think of. People joked about the lonely cousins in the realms where Tvíburi was hidden from sight, but while the gifts of nocturnal light and an immovable beacon to navigate by were great boons, if the world had instead been divided into the eternally sunlit and the eternally dark, neither half would have been grateful.

But the other benefits of Tvíbura's rotational allegiance were just as crucial. Only a single point at the center of the world could fall freely, surrendering completely to its mother's and sister's pull; the rest of the rock, ice and ocean that was dragged along with it was forced to compromise, struggling to hold together despite gravity's predilection for tugging harder on whatever happened to be nearest. And unlike the force wielded by Tvíburi, to which the world could accommodate once and for all, the sun's stretching and squeezing cycled relentlessly as it rose and set. The rock at the core grew hot from this endless kneading—which kept the ocean around it from freezing solid all the way down. The ocean, trapped between rock and ice, was forced to push hard against its confines, and the same gravitational edicts acting on the ice itself left it groaning and splintering. When the flaws in the ice lined up, the pressure of the water was enough to drive the ocean's riches all the way to the surface and beyond—restoring the air, and raining fresh, fertile soil down upon the land.

Freya paused to examine a dark smudge in the ice. But it was too diffuse to be a rootlet; it was just dirt, trapped beneath the now-compacted crystalline snow from some long-extinct geyser.

It took the strength of the sun itself and the rush of two worlds through the void to crack the ice and squeeze the ocean into the sky. The pause they were suffering was not from any lack of the usual forces; it could only be that the fractures required for a geyser were currently misaligned, present here and there at different depths but failing to meet up. If water *had* been finding a path to the surface lately, word of the event might not have reached the village—but the thicker, sweeter air it brought would have made itself known long ago.

Freya held the image of frustrated fissures in the back of her mind as she worked. Even if she'd identified the true nature of the problem, it was hard to imagine any way that a few thousand surface dwellers could influence the behavior of cracks in the ice so far beneath their feet.

A part of her counseled: *Time will fix it.* The geysers had flowed freely in the past, and if chance alone had stymied them, by chance alone they should return.

But how quickly? How certain could she be that any children she had wouldn't starve before the resurgence?

She looked up at Tvíburi. A slender white streak was clearly visible, rising up from the sunlit edge, bright enough to stand out against the sky. Their twin wasn't suffering from the same hiatus, but Freya didn't know if she should read this as a promise that the two worlds' fortunes would converge, or if Tvíburi was simply mocking her: flaunting the very thing her people needed, while knowing it was utterly beyond their reach.

∞

"THERE MUST BE life there, surely?" Freya asked her friends around the table. "If Tvíburi's made of the same ingredients as our world, experiencing the same conditions...?"

"I looked at it through a telescope once," Erna said. "At a traveling fair. You can see the geysers clearly, and the soil they've spread over the ice. That much seems to be the same."

"No farms?" Hanna joked.

"Farms might be a bit small to see, but I couldn't spot any grasslands either."

"I bet there are methanogens in the ocean," Gro declared. "Whether or not there are creatures on the surface."

"If the surface is barren," Bridget replied, "why wouldn't the ocean be barren too?"

Gro said, "Think how close these worlds are, and how long they've been together. How many chances would there have been, over the eons, for a geyser to blow spores all the way to Tvíburi?"

Freya laughed; she was not dismissing the idea, but it made her giddy. She said, "If that's true, why don't we follow them?"

This suggestion was enough to plunge the group into silence. Even Gro looked at her as if she'd lost her mind.

"What?" Freya protested. "If there *is* good air, and fertile soil..." She trailed off, unsure just what inspiring conclusion she'd thought she was reaching for. Quite apart from the absurdity of hoping that a band of explorers could cross the void like a spore on a water spout, if there had been geysers to ride there'd be no reason to ride them.

Erna said, "If we want a new geyser, maybe we should poison some roots. If they shrivel up faster than the ice reclaims the channel, it could leave a gap."

Freya was horrified, but Hanna had more practical concerns. "A gap all the way down to the ocean?" she asked.

Erna hesitated. "It would have to be."

"So you think we could more or less kill a whole Yggdrasil?" Hanna was incredulous. "You might as well talk about snuffing out the sun!"

"The upper roots are all too narrow anyway," Bridget added. "Even if they died and turned to dust, any water trying to take the same path would freeze before it reached the surface."

Erna didn't reply immediately, but nor did she seem willing to concede the argument.

"Anyone else know how to cure the world's problems?" Freya interjected. Some of their neighbors were casting worried glances at the group; the sooner they stopped talking about *poisoning roots*, the better.

"It's only been a day," Gro replied. "After a day, if you came to me covered in fresh soil and led me by the hand to the geyser it came from, I still wouldn't take you seriously."

∞

FREYA WOKE AND disentangled herself from her blankets, then lay on the floor of the tent for a moment. Twelve days into their collective endeavor, all of her friends had liberated at least one root from the ice, some of them two or three. Either she'd been unlucky, or she'd allowed her attention to wander. If she really had been negligent, today was the day to make up for it.

As she stumbled across the tent in the half light, she bumped into Bridget, but they exchanged nothing more than the grunts of acknowledgment that minimal civility required. No one was talkative in the mornings. Freya ate quickly, but when she started dressing for the ice she noticed that two of her brothers were stirring. "Go back to sleep, you idiots," she whispered, almost wishing they could understand her words, however disturbing that would have been. They kept reading the proximity of so many women as some kind of opportunity, when in truth it was the last thing on anyone's mind. Of all the customary prerequisites for conception, a guaranteed air supply was among the most prudent.

Freya left the tent and set out for the patch of ice she'd been allocated for the day. The advance party had pegged out rectangular sections before most of the searchers had arrived, so all she had to do was find the right marker for the corner of her latest piece of the grid. Above her, Tvíburi was little more than one-quarter lit—and when she took in the rising sun in the same view, her sense of longitude became an almost palpable thing, as if she'd physically paced her way west from the prime meridian where the twin would be perfectly bisected at dawn, watching the perspective shift along the way as it did for a nearer object if she merely leaned to the left or right. No doubt the lonely cousins were happy with their lives, but she would have felt bereft if she'd been forced to live beneath their flat, distant sky.

When she reached spike number seventy-three and looked out across the territory it marked, Freya's spirits sank. There was a plateau of blue ice rising up from the plain, occupying at least half of the patch. If the roots couldn't break the surface where she stood, what chance would they have to climb higher? So much for catching up with her friends' tallies.

It was hard not to feel cheated, but that was no excuse to shirk. Freya decided to ascend immediately and search the whole elevated region first. The approach was quite steep, and slippery with a lingering ethane dew; she had to use her pick a few times to give herself purchase.

When she reached the top of the plateau, she found that although the ice leveled off, it wasn't flat like the plain around it; the surface was dimpled and lumpy, rising and falling with every few strides. Freya had never encountered anything quite like it.

The dips in the ground held much more dirt than she was used to, but she worked assiduously to rake it aside.

In compensation, the mounds were much cleaner, though none of the ice itself was particularly clear: it was full of tiny defects that diffused the light, leaving it bluer, and much harder to inspect. She presumed it was newer than the ice of the plain; there hadn't been a geyser around here in living memory, but there might have been one recently enough that its accumulated snowfall had yet to be entirely leveled by erosion.

When she reached the drop at the far end of the plateau, she reversed, pacing out a parallel strip. The uneven terrain made every step different from the last; Freya could only hope that the novelty would help her keep her mind on the task, for whatever that was worth up here. She wasn't sure how long it would be from the time an active geyser refroze to the time a Yggdrasil would get around to sending roots through the new ice, but if there had once been a torrent of water shooting into the sky here, ripping up whatever had come before it, that could only lower her chances of success.

She arrived back at the edge where she'd started, and reversed again. She was beginning to view her lack of success with a degree of equanimity; she might be teased a little, but everyone knew her as a hard worker on the farm, and they all agreed that the tallies were mostly down to luck.

Freya stopped to rake the dirt out of a furrow. It was stickier than usual, and darker—not quite like soil, but not as loose and powdery as the fine gray dust that blew across the plain.

The rake met an obstruction. Freya kneeled down and started scooping the dirt aside with her hands. She could smell a buried fragrance rising from the furrow—several odors, in fact, some sweet, some pungent.

As the dirt parted from the thing it had concealed, she saw it plainly: a fully formed root flower, with six cooling petals arrayed around the central stalk. Freya laughed with delight; a shallow burial in such porous material probably hadn't been doing much to limit the flower's outgassing, so this didn't really count as a victory for the atmosphere, but it was still more than she'd expected to find. Why hadn't this root given up while the whole plateau was still above it, when so many others had barely made it within sight of the surface, down on the plain?

She spent a while savoring the discovery, brushing off as much of the clinging, aromatic dirt from the flower as she could, as if she were cleaning an old agricultural implement she'd chanced upon buried in a field. Then reluctantly, she rose to her feet and continued.

A few furrows later, she found a second flower, similarly buried in the dirt. Then a third, and a fourth. She was beginning to wonder if anyone would believe her when she reported the finds, even if she declined to claim them for her tally.

When the string of successes petered out, Freya wasn't surprised; the cluster must have come from rootlets branching off from a single, tenacious progenitor—one chance event out of sight to explain all four on the surface. Nonetheless, as she paced back and forth across the plateau three more times without another sighting, she found it harder to resign herself to the outcome than before, when she'd expected nothing.

And after one especially deep and dirt-filled furrow proved flowerless, her disappointment took hold of her. She swung her pick into the ice: six blows, a dozen, eighteen. She stopped, feeling foolish; she didn't have the time or energy to waste on pointless acts of frustration. And she very nearly walked on without even clearing away the shattered ice, but then that seemed doubly wasteful, so she squatted down and started pulling the shards out of the pit she'd made.

There was a root. She'd damaged the top of it with the pick, and it was seeping sweet-smelling alkanes onto the ice, but if she exposed some more of it, more carefully, there was no reason why the unbroken part wouldn't shed the injured section and flower.

When she was done, she went back to the previous barren furrow and attacked it. There was nothing to be found, at any depth she could reach. She went to the furrow before it, and tried again, stopping to remove the fragments of ice after each blow. There was a root not far below the surface— out of sight when she'd first looked, but the ice here could obscure anything.

By the time Freya had backtracked all the way to the fourth of the dirt-buried flowers, she'd exposed nine roots. She stopped to catch her breath, happy but bewildered. If the pattern continued, she'd have no hope of exposing every accessible root on the plateau before nightfall—which was glorious, but utterly perplexing. How could this much extra ice be anything but an obstacle? What was it that she didn't understand?

∞

"IT'S NOT ABOUT how far the roots have grown," Bridget argued. "It's about how hot or cold they are. If you pile up a lot of extra ice above the plain, that's going to trap the heat: if you dug down a couple of hand's breadths from the top of your plateau, you'd find it was every bit as warm as if you did the same anywhere on the plain. So the root tip isn't going to stop growing, just because it's come a long way from the ocean. It will only stop when it's cool enough."

"That makes sense," Freya conceded. "But it doesn't explain everything. The top layer of ice on that plateau has more roots in it than anyone's found on the plain. I can see why it might be the same, but...why *more?*" She looked around the table, trying to judge her friends' moods; she didn't want to annoy anyone by seeming to gloat about her find. But it was still too strange and wonderful to be treated as purely a matter of chance, requiring no further discussion.

Erna said, "You mentioned a lot of dirt in the furrows?"

"Yes."

"That would trap the heat even more, wouldn't it? And it would reflect less sunlight than bare ice."

"Right." Freya felt a little foolish now; everyone knew that dark objects grew warmer than lighter ones. "So maybe the real puzzle is why the furrows are so deep." Given their shape, it wasn't surprising that they filled up with dirt, but even if it would take eons for the whole plateau to be eroded away, it seemed odd that the wind hadn't yet sandblasted the top of it flat.

"I wonder what happens when a root flower is buried in a little valley like that," Gro mused. "I mean, it's still giving off methane and water vapor, but how freely does it all escape?"

Hanna said, "The methane would pass right through the dirt, but I think most of the water vapor would freeze on the grains of sand."

Freya looked at Gro, wondering if they were thinking the same thing. But if they were, Gro offered her the chance to speak first.

"The whole shape could be a kind of growth pattern," Freya said. "The dirt in the furrows traps water vapor from the root flowers as it turns to ice. That ice piles up, the furrows grow into mounds, and all the dirt that blows in on the wind spills off them onto the old mounds—which are now valleys and furrows themselves. And so it all starts again."

Hanna laughed. "So the roots keep re-burying themselves in ice made from the very water they're trying to get rid of! Which means they're raising the plateau higher and making their own job harder—but as long as there's enough dirt around to keep them warmer than they want to be, they'll keep trying to push their way up into the cold."

Gro said, "If that's really what's happening, I don't know if we should be surprised that it's the first time we've seen anything like it—or surprised that the phenomenon isn't so rare that no one's ever witnessed it at all."

Freya wasn't sure that they'd solved the mystery, but she doubted they'd come up with a better explanation if they sat around talking all night. Every scrap of food had vanished from the table long ago, and they'd all have to rise at the usual time in the morning.

She said, "To be honest, I haven't worked as hard as I did today since my first harvest. Whatever made the plateau the way it is, I'm going to need to get to sleep soon or I won't be able to face it again tomorrow."

Bridget said, "You do know that we're all coming with you, to help?"

Freya glanced at the others, but they seemed to be in agreement. "What about your own patches?" she asked.

"We'll return to them when the plateau's done," Hanna replied. "If that's where the roots are, that's where our time's best spent. No one expects you to break your back trying to get through all the work up there, alone."

∞

AS THE FIVE friends set off across the ice together, Freya wondered if her companions were sufficiently awake yet to hear the wild thoughts that had kept her from sleep. She wasn't even sure that she was in any state herself to decide what was worth repeating. As she'd lain on the blankets with her limbs aching, picturing the roots that stretched down to the buried ocean beneath her, the ideas that flowed through her head had seemed urgent and compelling—for all the uncertainties, and all the questions they raised. By daylight, the case was not so clear.

But when the blue ice of the plateau came into sight ahead of them, she realized that she had no hope of remaining silent all day, and it would be better to speak and be ridiculed now than to interrupt her friends when they were trying to work.

"If we placed mounds of black sand over the ice in the right pattern," she asked, "do you think we could grow a plateau like this somewhere else?"

"I don't see why not," Bridget replied, managing to sound both intrigued and annoyed—as if she resented being forced to think about anything when the sun had barely cleared the horizon, but found the idea too enticing to ignore. "If you covered a big enough area, there'd probably be some roots positioned in the right place to get things started. It might take a while, but maybe it would be worth it, just to be ready for the next solar flares."

"I'm thinking about more than the flares," Freya confessed. "With the natural version, in the end most of the dirt will get stuck in the ice or blown away…but if people were actively tending the surface, who knows how high we could make the plateau?"

Gro said, "I think I know where you're heading with this."

"You do?" Freya waited, hoping to be spared the humiliation of having to spell it out herself if Gro had already decided that the idea was preposterous.

"Raise a tall enough mountain," Gro guessed, "and the sheer weight of it will start to create new fractures. What better way to encourage more geysers?"

Freya wasn't sure how to reply. If it was true that the ice would crack all the way to the ocean under the kind of load she was imagining, that would be the perfect outcome. But it would be dishonest of her to take credit for it. It wasn't what she'd had in mind at all.

"That might happen," she said. "But can we be sure that it would?"

Hanna said, "That depends on how long you can keep adding more ice."

"Suppose we can coax the roots into doing the job for as long as we like," Freya replied. "Keep the tips warm, so they can't tell that they're already high above the surface, and keep capturing all the water vapor they put out."

Hanna grunted irritably. "If there's no limit to how high you go, then of course the mountain's going to break the ice *eventually.* You might as well pick a number, tell me to start counting, then ask if I'll ever reach a number greater than yours."

Erna said, "That's not true."

"It's basic arithmetic!" Hanna retorted.

"It's basic arithmetic that counting takes you past any given number," Erna agreed, "but the comparison is false. Just because the height of a mountain increases without bounds, that doesn't mean its weight will do the same."

Hanna was silent for a while, then she conceded, "You're right."

Bridget said, "What?"

"Gravity is stronger close-up," Hanna replied. "The farther you go above the world, the weaker its pull will be."

"Yes," Bridget agreed, "but it never goes away completely."

Hanna said, "It does, when Tvíburi's gravity cancels it out and starts pulling in the other direction."

"Who said anything about putting the mountain right below Tvíburi?" Bridget protested.

"Nobody." Erna was amused. "That's not the argument I had in mind! Though if you want to put the mountain there, that will only help make it lighter."

Freya kept quiet; her friends were doing all the work for her, and any contribution she could make would be superfluous.

But now Hanna was confused. "How does the mountain not grow heavier, if you don't use Tvíburi?"

Erna said, "What's one, plus a quarter, plus a ninth, plus a sixteenth…and so on, forever?"

"I have no idea," Hanna replied.

"Nor do I," Erna admitted, "but if I had to guess, I'd say it's less than two, and I'm sure it doesn't grow without bounds. The weight of a mountain would be like that—at least until it grew so tall that its own gravity started to affect the result as much as the gravity of the world itself."

"I think we can rule that out," Bridget said dryly. "However eager the roots are to oblige us, they're not going to drain the whole ocean."

"No." Erna turned to Freya. "But it's your mountain, after all. Where do you want to put it?"

"Right under Tvíburi," Freya confessed.

Gro said, "That makes no sense! Why reduce the weight?"

The group had almost reached the plateau. Freya was having second thoughts; perhaps she should accept the alibi Gro was offering her, and be done with her own madness.

But she couldn't stop herself.

"If we *can* break the ice and make new geysers, the job would be done," she said. "But if that doesn't work, if the ice bears the weight...then maybe we can build a mountain that takes us halfway to Tvíburi."

Her companions became quiet. Freya listened to their footsteps crunching through the powdered ice, grateful that at least no one had fallen to the ground laughing.

"Why only halfway?" Hanna asked.

Freya wasn't sure if the question was meant sarcastically, but she took it in good faith. "Tvíburi isn't perfectly still in the sky," she replied. "It moves slightly nearer and farther away, and even turns its face a little. If we tried to make a solid bridge of ice all the way between the worlds, it would just snap."

"All right. But why stop at the halfway point? Why not get closer? Three quarters? Nine tenths?"

Freya said, "I suspect that ice is like most things: better at holding together when you squeeze it than when you pull on it. We know it can take a lot of weight pushing down on it—but imagine a column of ice, as tall as the two worlds are distant, just hanging from the sky above Tvíburi. I think it would break long before it reached that size. And even if I'm mistaken, I doubt that the root tips would keep growing in the same direction once gravity was telling them they were headed down, not up."

"I can't argue with any of that," Hanna declared. "But it makes the next question more painful."

Freya said, "Do your worst."

"What possible use would it be, to go only halfway? If we could travel to Tvíburi itself, it might have the best soil and the thickest air we could hope for. But halfway through the void, there won't even be air. We'd struggle to survive for a day! What would be the point of getting there?"

Freya had lain awake contemplating exactly that problem. "I can't be sure," she said. "But we'd be closer to Tvíburi, and we wouldn't just be staring up at it, hoping for some impossible magic to raise us into the sky. Instead, we'd be staring down at it, hoping for something less magical: a way to descend. There are lizards that glide down from the tallest cliffs—and a few crazy people have mimicked them, riding contraptions that use the same principles."

Bridget said, "But even from a cliff, it's dangerous, and you can't take much more with you than your own body. If you want to relocate *whole villages* to Tvíburi…"

"I know," Freya replied. "But if we could send a dozen people across, with enough supplies to get started, that would be something. They could found a new village on their own. Then at least life would go on, however bad things became on Tvíbura."

From the silence that followed, it was clear that no one took much comfort from that prospect.

Freya said, "Or, Tvíburi might have Yggdrasils too, and then the people who crossed over could start raising their own mountain. If we could grow two separate mountains, both reaching into the void, we might be able to join them with a bridge of ropes, long and flexible enough to survive the changing positions of its endpoints. Then we'd have a path all the way from the surface of Tvíbura to the surface of her twin. And if the fortunes of one world fell while the other's rose, we could take our pick between them."

2 ~~~~~~

FREYA stood outside the meeting hall, hugging herself in a vain attempt to ward off the chill of the night air, gazing in through the windows at the crowd gathered in the lamplit room.

Britt emerged. "I was wondering where you'd gotten to. We're ready for you."

"All right."

"Don't look so worried! We always treat our guests with respect," Britt assured her.

Freya followed her into the hall. There were about eighty people present—mostly standing, with a few seats for the elderly and infirm. At least that was likely to discourage most of her audience from dozing off, while forcing her to put her case as succinctly as possible. If she kept people on their feet too long, their patience would run out very quickly.

She took the speaker's position at the front of the hall. "Thank you for welcoming me into your village," she began. "And thank you for coming here tonight, to hear the reasons for my visit."

Freya had been intending to open with a reminder about the diminishing yields that everyone was facing, but as she took in some of the gaunter figures in front of her, it suddenly felt both superfluous, and too bleak a beginning. She wanted her potential allies thinking about their own strengths, as much as their problems—and something her host had told her over breakfast had remained with her all day.

"I believe that many young people in this village, before settling into adult life, follow the tradition of the Great Walk: taking thirty days to trek the whole way around Tvíbura. I must confess that I've never made that journey myself, though I expect to cover a similar distance soon, as I travel back and forth seeking help with the endeavor that I'm here to talk about tonight. But since so many of you have the experience of setting out from your home one day, heading west, vowing never to turn around until you find yourself back where you started... that seems like the perfect measure of just how great a feat any one of us can accomplish. One and a half million strides! When I speak those words, it sounds impossible. But you know that it isn't. All of you here have done it, or know someone who has."

She paused to gauge the effect of her words. The reception so far appeared friendly, but some people were already fidgeting; they had better things to do than listen to her flattery.

"One and a half million strides," she said, "is *twice* the distance from this village to the nearest point on the surface of Tvíburi! And I'm here to ask for your support to make a new kind of Great Walk possible, perhaps for the great-grandchildren of the youngest people here in this room. I want to start growing a mountain of ice that will reach up toward Tvíburi, as the first step toward making it possible for our descendants to travel there, live there, and farm there, almost as easily as they would walk to new farmland on our own world."

Some people were gawping incredulously now, but others were smiling at the audacity of the scheme, and no one was fidgeting anymore.

Freya described the plateau she'd found out on the ice field, then sketched her plans for a faster-growing, artificially sculpted version. "We would need to make this mountain hollow, both to keep it light and to provide a route for travelers once the air out on the slope became too thin. But we would also need to partition it, building floors along the way to catch the air that the roots release, lest it all fall to the bottom and leave the upper reaches of the mountain no different from the uninhabitable void." She was honest about the uncertainties, both in the construction process, and the ultimate usefulness of the result. "Will there be a safe way to fall from such a height, on to Tvíburi? We can't know that, until we've tried to fall on to Tvíbura from a similar height. Will there be Yggdrasils on Tvíburi with roots rising up through the ice, allowing us to grow a twin for this mountain and bridge the gap in comfort? We can't know that, until the bravest of our descendants have set foot on that world to learn the answer for themselves."

She stopped and asked for questions. For a moment everyone in the audience seemed dazed, and as they broke their polite silence and began to talk among themselves, Freya prepared herself for the usual objections. Surely the roots would stop growing? Surely the mountain would topple to the ground?

"You say the mountain might crack the ice beneath it, bringing new geysers?" an elderly woman asked.

"Yes. That's always possible."

"But you'd be taking steps to spread the load, and to make the mountain as light as you can?" The woman's tone was puzzled, verging on reproachful.

"Yes," Freya admitted. "Some of my friends have chosen the opposite tactic: they aim to build a mountain that works like a pick, with its weight concentrated on the smallest foundations possible. They hope to raise it at the western setting point, where Tvíburi does nothing to lessen the mountain's weight."

"Tell them to come here," the woman replied. "What we need are fresh geysers, not some nonsense about a ladder to the sky. I'd happily vote for my farm to help feed them."

"I understand," Freya said. "But they've chosen a place where the gravity will give them an advantage." In fact, they would have gained even more weight at the poles, but the selection of the site was further complicated by the way the sun tugged on the ocean; at the poles, it was never pulling water toward the surface. "They're not going to make their job harder by trying the same thing here."

"Then perhaps we'll do it ourselves," the woman retorted. "We're not afraid of work, and the world can't have too many geysers."

"That's true," Freya agreed cautiously. "But the trouble is, we don't know if it's possible to create them that way. If it turns out not to be, all the work will have been for nothing, and it might be too late to try anything else."

A younger woman, further back in the crowd, joined the discussion. "Then raise a mountain here that does its best to break the ice, and if it fails, it will still be in the right place to reach toward Tvíburi."

"It's not that simple," Freya replied. "The two aims are so different that they shape the designs in different ways, even from the start. A mountain built to exert the greatest possible pressure at its base will not make a safe bridge, even if it fails to crack the ice to the depth needed to bring forth new geysers. Who in good conscience would send travelers across the largest bridge ever built, if its shape was a compromise—a way of making do, a way of patching over the failure of an entirely different structure, with entirely different needs?"

The older of her two interlocutors was undeterred. "Then do what you like, wherever you like, but don't expect us to feed you! Unless you're offering a chance to bring back the geysers, you're not worth taking food out of the mouths of my grandchildren!"

Freya lowered her gaze, chastened. The woman's position was understandable—and there was no point repeating one more time that the best-designed mountain for the purpose she sought might fail to crack the ice, when it was equally true that Freya's own version might fail to be of any use at all.

∞

WHEN THE MEETING was over, Freya stayed in the hall and shared a meal with Britt and half a dozen of the other villagers. They were all polite, and almost apologetic that she'd come so far only to be rebuffed, but none of them were willing to vote for their own farms to contribute food or supplies to her project.

"Things are tight," Aslaug explained, contemplating the less-than-lavish feast that they'd prepared for their visitor.

"Which is why I'm doing this," Freya replied, trying not to let her exasperation spill over into discourtesy.

"But no one believes they'll stay that way," Britt added. "We've always come through the quiet times in the past."

"There were less of us in the past. And what if the quiet times are growing longer?" Freya was beginning to wish she'd taken this more somber line with the whole gathering.

But it showed no sign of working on her present audience. "Everything's cyclic," Hetty declared confidently. "Can you name *one thing* in nature that goes just one way?"

Freya said, "If one example would be enough to kill us, why would I expect to be able to do that?"

Everyone around the table smiled, trying without success to conceal their amusement. Her words were empty sophistry. Her intentions might be noble, her purpose sincere, but nothing she'd said had been the least bit persuasive.

∞

FREYA LAY AWAKE between the blankets on the floor of Britt's guest room. She was close enough to the window that she could see the bright edge of Tvíburi, protruding past the gutter that ran along the side of the roof above her. It was hard to sleep with her brothers fighting, wrestling with each other, mewling and hissing.

When Freya had been a child, she'd been sure that she knew all three as individuals—not by tracking their locations from moment to moment, but by recognizing their idiosyncratic temperaments. But now she was far less confident that this told her anything. If one of the erstwhile subjugated pair succeeded in upending the hierarchy, would she be able to tell the difference, or would the result be indistinguishable to her? She wasn't even sure that the brothers themselves had any sense of their identity that ran deeper than their awareness of their own current status. If a jealous pretender finally usurped the previous proud-but-wary ruler, would he know or feel anything that his predecessor hadn't known or felt?

Britt said, "Are you awake?"

Freya rolled over and peered toward the doorway, where her host appeared in silhouette against the gray of the hall behind her. "Yes. What is it?"

"We're too inbred in this place," Britt replied.

For a moment Freya thought she was apologizing for her fellow villagers' lack of foresight, but then a low howl and a palpable thump against the inside of her abdomen reminded her that the fighting had probably not gone unnoticed outside the confines of her body.

"Are you sure that's what you want?" she asked.

"We can't all stop having children until the geysers return."

Freya laughed wearily. "No, we can't."

"We don't have a lot of visitors from as far away as you've come," Britt explained. "I tried to get pregnant when I did my Great Walk, but I must have had bad luck." She shifted tentatively in the doorway.

Freya said, "If you're resolved to try again now, you're welcome." *Anything to quieten these idiots down.*

Britt approached and knelt down on the edge of the blankets. "I haven't done this for a while," Freya confessed.

"Were there any children from the other times?"

"No. But I was young, and I think my brothers were so evenly matched then that they got in each other's way."

The two of them worked in silence for a while, trying to get into position, while whoever had won the fight in Freya's belly moaned impatiently. Britt's own brothers were quiet, recognizing the nature of the situation, but Freya remained wary; she'd heard stories about women surprised by an unexpected reversal.

Freya closed her eyes and felt the dominant brother begin protruding. She forced herself to relax and let him emerge unhindered. It was uncomfortable at first, from sheer lack of practice, but she'd be unwise to flinch now if she ever wanted to face childbirth.

When something close to half of the brother's body was inside her, Britt began to sigh. Freya held the woman's shoulders, bemused as ever by this intimacy in which she was almost, but not quite, a participant. At least there were no embarrassing mutinous tussles to complicate the exchange; whatever their long-term aspirations, the losing pair from the night's ruckus seemed to have accepted their place, for now.

When it was over, Britt rested her face on Freya's shoulder while Freya's brother withdrew, then the two women parted and lay side by side on the blanket.

"Do you know if your own brothers have had children?" Freya asked.

Britt said, "I think so, but I'm not sure. That's part of what went wrong on my Great Walk—they had to have it their way."

"That must have been annoying."

Britt took her hand and squeezed it. "I'm sorry you didn't get what you wanted here."

Freya said, "Well, at least I've made one of my brothers happy. If only there were some favor he could do in return."

Britt snickered. "Plow a field? Help with the harvest?"

"I'm sure there's a children's story where someone was in trouble—injured out on the ice...or maybe captured by their enemies?—and they sent their brother crawling off for help."

She was joking, but Britt didn't reply. Freya pulled her hand free and turned to face the window. Maybe it was time for some new stories, where Tvíburi wasn't Tvíbura's twin, but the mother of her brother's child.

She closed her eyes. There had to be words that would work, that would make it happen—or at least make it possible. But she hadn't found them yet.

3 〰〰〰

WHEN Freya saw that the fair was in town, she almost turned around and walked back onto the ice. No one would be interested in hearing her talk about the death of their crops when there were far more cheerful diversions to be had.

But the wind was relentless, and she hadn't eaten for days. Even with the fair competing for the villagers' time and generosity, they would never refuse food and shelter to a traveler.

The wind whipped gray sand around her feet, stinging her through the cloth of her trousers, and as she reached the first paved street she realized that the dusty barrage was coming from the village itself, not blowing in across the ice. She'd seen this kind of thing a few times before, when the soil that had supported a whole swathe of farmland suddenly lost its ability to cohere. The ring of roads and buildings that encircled the farms was usually enough to act as both a barrier against the wind and a trap for drifting soil, to the point where at least the bulk of it could be contained and brought back to the fields. But there seemed to be some threshold where the over-cropped soil became so loose and light that nothing could be done to hold on to it.

The fair had set up its tents at the western edge of the village, and as Freya trudged around the ring road, the sound of people talking and laughing rose and fell with the wind. Normally, a villager would have stopped to greet her by now and ask where she'd come from, but there was no one in sight. Everyone was at the fair.

She approached the cluster of tents reluctantly. She was tired, and even if she'd been in the mood to spend time gazing at the exhibits she had nothing to offer in payment. All she could do was try to find a corner out of the wind and hope that an observant local would realize that she had no connection to the fair. Freya had never been too proud to accept the kind of hospitality that she'd offer any traveler who came to her own village, but it would be humiliating if she had to explain herself in order to make her situation clear.

She weaved between the tents, squeezing past queues of people waiting to enter, and found herself on a patch of ground that was open to the sky but sheltered from all sides. In the middle of this square, a woman stood by a telescope, touting for customers. "See the mountains and ravines of Tvíburi! See the geysers of molten ice, close enough to touch!"

Freya found a place to stand where she wasn't blocking any-one's way, and put her dusty pack on the ground. The telescope woman turned toward her and smiled. Freya nodded a greeting, but kept her distance; it would be rude to approach, as if she were a potential customer, only to plead poverty at the last moment.

As the afternoon wore on, the other touts seemed to be drawing ever larger crowds, but the telescope remained unvisited. Freya glanced up at the waxing crescent, wondering why no one seemed interested.

The telescope woman approached her. "I'm Inga."

"Freya."

"You're not from this village, are you?"

"No."

"Do you want to take a look?" Inga offered cheerfully.

"I…" Freya lowered her gaze, ashamed.

"No charge for a fellow traveler," Inga assured her.

Freya followed her over to the instrument, and lay down on the bench beneath the eyepiece. She wasn't sure why she had never done this before; maybe as a child, other attractions had grabbed her attention first, and by the time a closer look at Tvíburi had begun to seem alluring she'd spent what her mother had to spare.

She squirmed across the bench and squinted into the eyepiece, trying to turn the confusing puddle of light she was seeing into something sharper. "I can't…" she complained. But then she craned her neck and suddenly, she could.

The view showed an expanse of pale blue ice, covered in fine fractures like the lines on an old woman's skin.

"Use the wheels," Inga urged her. She guided Freya's hand to a pair of disks with corrugated edges, connected to shafts on the telescope's mount. "Turn the top one to move the view from side to side, the other to move it up and down, as you're seeing it."

Freya swung the telescope to the left too fast, transforming the landscape into a blur, but when it became still again she was staring down at a canyon. "Have you ever seen anything like that on Tvíbura?" she asked, before realizing that Inga would have no idea what she was looking at. "A furrow in the ice so deep?"

"No," Inga replied. "We're flatter, for sure."

Freya nudged the wheels, searching the ice for a deposit of soil. Finally, she was rewarded: a deep brown splotch, piled up in the middle, tall enough to cast a shadow. As far as she could tell, it was barren, with no trace of wild grasses. But did that mean the soil itself was incapable of supporting life, or simply that the right kind of plants had never arrived, or arisen, on Tvíburi? It was certainly sticky enough to have held together despite the lack of vegetation; that alone made it seem more promising than the gray dust here that was blowing away on the wind.

She slid off the bench, afraid of becoming engrossed in the view and outstaying her welcome. "Thank you," she said. "I'm glad I saw that."

"It's easy to take Tvíburi for granted." Inga glanced around the square at the oblivious fair-goers. "Half the world has spent their lives looking up at it, but some people think that means there's nothing more to see."

"Believe me, that's not how I feel." Freya hesitated, reluctant to burden this woman with the details of her increasingly unlikely ambitions. But even if Inga had no crops of her own to offer to a team of mountain-builders, she was entitled to know what could be done in the face of dwindling yields and desiccated soil. If nothing changed, her grandchildren would starve even sooner than those of any farmer.

Freya said, "I think we need to build a bridge."

Inga listened attentively, and if she seemed to be struggling to keep herself from interrupting, she had the demeanor, not of an exasperated skeptic eager to declare the whole idea preposterous, but of someone who kept anticipating both problems and solutions, who was waiting to hear whether the speaker would eventually catch up with her.

By the time Freya finally stopped talking, she must have addressed most of those concerns, because Inga just smiled and said, "That has to be the most intrepid plan I've ever heard."

"I'll take that as a compliment," Freya replied. "Though I'm not sure it's the kind of endorsement that would recommend the idea to many farmers."

"So you're traveling from village to village, trying to get support?"

"Yes."

"Any luck?"

"About as much as you're having with your telescope."

Inga frowned. "Why? Do people not believe that any of this is possible...or do they not believe that it could help?"

Freya explained about Gro's competing project. "Everyone wants that to work instead. A better result, and a faster one— if it happens at all. But it makes my own plans sound like a waste of time."

Inga pondered this. "You need props," she said.

"I need what?"

"Objects that help you demonstrate your point. You need to make it easier for people to see why even the tallest mountain might not create a geyser."

Freya said, "How can I make people *see* something that I'm not even certain of myself?"

"You're not certain—but do you think your doubts about your friend's scheme are well-founded, or do you think you're just too stubborn to give up on your own idea?"

Freya was bemused. "Can anyone answer a question like that?"

Inga said, "If your doubts are well-founded, there must be something you can do to get them across to other people." She glanced away; someone was finally approaching her telescope. "Meet me here when the fair closes, and I'll see what I can do to help."

∞

FREYA PASSED THE time walking around the fairgrounds, trying to keep warm, too embarrassed to start approaching people and beg them for food and shelter. If anything, she tried to remain inconspicuous; if a villager did offer her hospitality now, how would she keep her appointment with Inga?

Halfway between sunset and midnight, as the laneways between the tents started emptying, she made her way back to the telescope. Inga still had one young customer, but when the girl left—beaming at what she'd seen—Inga gestured to Freya to approach.

"We're here for two more days, so I won't be packing this up," she explained. "I just have to cover it to protect it from the dust." She took some sheets of heavy fabric out of a box, unfolded them, and pegged them in place over the telescope.

She led Freya through the fairgrounds to a small, drab tent, and lit a lamp just inside the entrance. Most of the space within was taken up by two carts, piled high with wooden crates.

"How do you people lug all this across the ice?" Freya wondered.

"It's not that hard, if you know what you're doing; once you've got the wheels rolling, the carts only need an occasional push. The most dangerous part is when we have to stop in a hurry— that's when I wish things had more weight and less momentum." Inga was rummaging through one of the carts as she spoke, but then she stopped and announced happily, "Here it is!"

She carried the box she'd found away from the cart and placed it on the floor of the tent, then opened it and began removing some of its contents. "The first thing you want to impress on people is that, no matter how much ice you pile up, there's a limit to how much it will weigh."

Freya accepted that, but Erna's mumbling about "one plus a quarter plus a ninth" didn't really translate into anything she could sell with conviction to a room full of farmers. "Impress is a strong word."

Inga was fiddling with some contraption from her crate. "Every child learns the inverse-square law, though?"

"Yes," Freya agreed. "But the law itself is one thing; all its consequences are another."

"So you need to make this consequence visible," Inga replied. She took the gadget and offered it to Freya. It was a long tank with a square cross-section, and a flexible partition inside. The partition was connected to a series of pegs that protruded through holes in the side of the tank and emerged along an attached board, on which a grid had been drawn, its intervals marked with numbers.

"Set the pegs to the inverse-square law," Inga instructed.

"I don't understand," Freya confessed.

"The first peg is the number one, for a distance of one. The inverse square of one is one, so make the height of the part that sticks out equal to one."

"All right." Freya did as she'd been told. "But the next peg isn't 'two'; there are six pegs before the next number."

Inga said, "So the next peg is seven-sixths, and the inverse square of that is thirty-six forty-ninths. If you raise the peg almost halfway between four sixths and five sixths that will be close enough."

"You expect my would-be investors to juggle fractions like this?" Freya joked.

"They won't have to fret about the details," Inga promised. "You just have to get things right yourself, and then show them a nice smooth curve along the tops of the pegs that passes through all the easy points that they can check themselves if they want to."

Freya kept at it, until all the pegs were set—with the last one barely protruding at all.

"And this tells us...?" she wondered.

Inga handed her a flask full of ethane. "Fill it up," she said.

Freya tipped ethane into the tank, into the space between one wall and the partition now shaped by her carefully positioned pegs.

"Now pour it all from *there* into *here*," Inga suggested, passing Freya a much smaller, unadorned and unmodified tank, cubical in shape.

"Will it fit?" Freya wondered.

"Go ahead and see."

Freya raised the larger tank and drained it carefully into the smaller one. There was no overflow; if anything, a narrow gap remained at the top of the second tank.

The two tanks had the same square cross-section, but though the first tank was eleven times longer in total, the volume that remained below the inverse-square curve of the partition was no more than that of the single cube.

Inga said, "So the weight of a mountain whose peak is *twelve times* farther from the center of the world than the ground is would actually weigh very slightly less than a mountain that only stretched from the ground to a height twice as far from the center of the world...if in the latter case, gravity didn't vary with distance at all."

Freya was confused for a moment, but then she understood. "People have no experience of gravity growing weaker. Our intuition comes from such a small range of heights that we can only imagine the weight of objects that obey the rules we actually see—where piling up a stack of rocks doesn't mean the top few rocks weigh less than the bottom ones."

"Exactly." Inga took the small tank from her and placed it on the ground. "But now you still have to persuade them that a mountain of ice as tall as the center of the world is deep—with every portion weighing what it would at ground-level—might not be heavy enough to break the crust of ice beneath it."

"How am I supposed to do that?"

Inga said, "Show them exactly how strong ice is, and how little it weighs. You can't show them the mountain they need to imagine, but you can show them something smaller, supported by a smaller crust."

"So...I just use two slabs of ice in the same proportion to each other? Like a map drawn to scale?"

Inga thought it over. "Not quite. If you shrink everything by the same amount, the weight of the load gets smaller faster than the area of the ice resisting that weight: the area of the vertical plane separating the adjacent regions in the crust that the load is trying to shear apart. So you actually need to exaggerate the size of the mountain compared to the depth of the crust, in order to make a fair demonstration of the necessary strength."

Freya said, "Some people won't understand that. It will look like I'm cheating."

Inga was amused. "But not in favor of your own argument! If anything, it will look as if you're being unfair on yourself, and trying too hard to break the crust."

So she should try, not excessively hard, but fairly. Freya wanted to know the truth; if she'd been wasting her time that would be a painful thing to learn—but better to find out now than keep wandering from village to village when she ought to be helping her friends achieve their own saner and more modest goals.

"I don't really know exactly how I should scale things," she admitted.

"Let me think," Inga replied. "I promise you, we get a good enough education in the science of forces and motion to keep our acrobats safe, but you're calling on ideas I don't use every day." She closed her eyes, grimacing. "The height of the ground-level equivalent for an infinite mountain would be two hundred and fifty thousand strides—the same as the distance to the center of the world. Most people agree that the crust is at least one tenth as deep. If we want something smaller that gives a fair test of the strength of ice, we need to keep a constant ratio between the volume of ice in the load, and the area resisting the shear. So, whatever scales we apply to the height and width of the mountain, we need to apply *both* of them to the depth of the crust."

"All right." Freya was hanging on to the argument, just barely. "So for a start, we need to know the width of the mountain?"

"Yes."

"The one my friends are considering would be a thousand strides across," Freya recalled.

"So what's a manageable mountain for an exhibit?" Inga mused. "It need not be as tall and skinny as the imaginary one. Maybe two strides tall, and one stride wide?"

"All right." Freya didn't want to think about the logistics of rolling such a cylinder from village to village, but if she pleaded to make the toy mountain any smaller, she feared the toy crust would end up thinner than a knife blade.

"So all in all, we need to scale the crust by one hundred and twenty-five million." Inga laughed. "That brings it down to one five-thousandth of a stride."

"That's not going to work," Freya concluded glumly.

"No, it's impractical," Inga agreed. "No lenses I've ever made are that thin. We need to multiply by five, at least: make the crust one thousandth of a stride deep, and the mountain ten strides tall."

"Ten!" Freya didn't think she'd ever seen an artificial structure ten strides tall; even the largest of the fair's tents probably fell short of that by a stride or two. "It was kind of you to give this so much thought, but what you're describing is completely beyond me."

Inga said, "You want to build a bridge between worlds, but not a tower ten strides tall?"

"I don't have the tools," Freya replied. "I don't even have a cart."

Inga stood silently in the lamplight for a while, weighing up the problem. "This is important, isn't it?" she said finally. "One way or the other. I've seen what some of the farms are like. We need new geysers, or we need to reach Tvíburi."

"That's what I believe."

"Then you'd better come and meet the others," Inga decided. "And see if we can talk them into it."

Freya said, "Talk them into what?"

Inga smiled. "Letting you join the fair, along with a new exhibit: either a tower of ice that weighs so much it might as well be infinite, supported by a sheet of ice a fraction of its height…or a tower of ice that shatters that support, and shows us the way to make geysers. But whichever it is, it will be in aid of something marvelous: a bridge to Tvíburi, or the pick to end all picks, rising up from the ice field into the sky."

∞

FREYA WATCHED FROM the ground as Inga and Naja fitted the final level to the scaffolding. She hated standing by when other people were working, but her new friends had spent half their lives performing similar tasks, and she'd already slowed down the construction too much by getting in the way and trying to learn everything at once.

"Done!" Naja called down, before jumping off the edge of the platform. Inga took the ladder, and she had advised Freya to do the same. "Falling eight or ten strides is painless—and mildly entertaining the first few times—but your older self will thank you for protecting your knees from unnecessary jolts."

Inga and Freya rolled the last piece of the column over the ice field to the edge of the structure, and maneuvered it into the sling. Freya's hands were still tender from the dozens of small cuts she'd acquired while learning to carve a roughly hewn slab into a cylinder like this. But the version in front of them now had been rolled back and forth over five different grades of abrasive sand, to the point where it was almost smooth. Inga had promised that if they went ahead and took the exhibition to the public, she'd show Freya how to give the cylinders a near-optical polish, so they gleamed in the sunlight.

While the two of them hauled on the pulley rope together, Naja climbed the ladder beside the ascending cylinder, steadying it and making sure it didn't slip or start swinging. They were lucky: there was almost no wind today.

When the cylinder reached the top platform, Naja adjusted the ropes connected to the sling so that Freya and Inga's next few pulls would make the thing vertical. Then they clamped the rope and rested for a moment, before taking the ladder to join Naja.

"This is it!" Inga marveled. "Once we add this piece, the tower will be as good as infinite."

Freya remained silent; she didn't know what she was hoping for any more. The work had proved so exhausting that by the time they were raising the third piece, she'd been desperately willing the surrogate crust to shatter, just to spare her any more labor. And if it had happened then, or with the addition of the fourth, the result might have been convincing enough to persuade her that Gro's project was the only one to back.

But if it happened now? Nobody knew exactly how thick the real crust was, or what other errors their imperfect model might contain. If their mock-infinite tower broke its supporting base, that would be enough to put an end to any hope of proceeding with the bridge, but Freya would be dead long before it was certain that geysers could be summoned this way.

The three of them worked together, unhooking the cylinder from the vertical rope that had raised it and attaching it to the horizontal loop that would carry it for the last stage of its journey. Freya imagined a crowd of spectators below, some of them still hoping to win prizes for guessing the correct breaking point, or wagering on the crust's invincibility.

"Won't word of the result spread between the villages?" she'd asked Inga.

"It will, but no one will believe what they haven't seen with their own eyes. People will bet on their own instincts about the forces at play here, not someone else's claims that contradict those feelings."

Freya tugged on the rope, while Inga and Naja walked beside the cylinder toward the hole in the center of the platform, from which a stubby portion of the existing tower could be seen protruding. When the new piece was hanging right over its four predecessors—each one a little narrower than the last—Freya joined them. If something went wrong in this final stage, the more hands there were to steady the tower, the better their chances would be to keep it from toppling.

"Ready?" Inga asked, kneeling down at one side of the cylinder while Naja kneeled at the opposite point.

"Yes," Freya replied.

Inga spoke a brief, guttural word in the fair's dialect that had no precise translation, though its present usage was transparent: as she finished uttering it, she and Naja simultaneously sliced through two cords at the bottom of the sling, which were holding its two halves together. The tensed, elastic structure snapped apart and the cylinder began to descend.

The final piece of the column had barely a thumb's breadth to fall. It landed squarely in place with a thud, and with the sling clear of the impact. Freya waited, arms spread, ready to respond as Inga and Naja climbed to their feet. But nothing had skewed the release, and as far as she could tell the cylinder wasn't shaking or swaying at all. Let alone falling.

They'd placed the thin sheet of ice that was supporting the whole structure on top of two square blocks half a stride high, and two strides apart. If that crust cracked and the base of the tower dropped to the ground, the effect would not be subtle. But so far, it was holding.

The three of them stood motionless for a while, their eyes fixed on the top of the tower. Then Inga said, "Let's go down and see what's happening."

As they walked across the platform, Freya kept looking back, expecting the cylinder to plummet at any moment. She was last onto the ladder, and she gripped the side rails tightly, prepared for the scaffolding to lurch wildly if the tower collapsed, with the five pieces tumbling as they fell, crashing into the beams around them.

Back on the ground, as they approached the sheet of ice, Freya would have sworn she could discern a subtle change in its shape. But when it came to her turn to squat down and inspect the graduated rods beside it, there was no sign that it had sagged, buckled or bent. No cracks or flaws had appeared. The strain of holding up the completed tower was not enough to deform it to any measurable degree, let alone tear it apart.

Freya remained as she was, too unsteady to rise, but Inga reached down and clasped her shoulder. She said, "It's starting to look as if my great-grandchildren might just get a chance to visit Tvíburi."

4 〜〜〜〜

GRO finished her inspection of the double doors at the top of the stairs. "One down, twenty-six to go," she said.

Freya glanced over her shoulder at the next platform they'd be visiting. The slanted legs of the would-be tripod had come a long way toward their meeting point, but though the straight-line distance between the tops of the columns was barely fifty strides now, the trip down to the ground then up again would take at least half a day. "I won't be happy until the ice has grown around the frames, and we can check that the gap can be made airtight," she replied. All they'd shown so far was that the doors themselves, and the box between them, wouldn't leak.

Gro gathered up her tools into her pack, and motioned for Freya to go before her. There was something dreamlike about stepping through a door whose frame was surrounded by thin air, into a dark wooden box, and emerging through a second unwalled doorway to confront a flight of stairs so long that its lower reaches were impossible to perceive, shrunken by perspective into a crack in the side of the tripod's leg.

Freya hooked her safety ropes onto the stair rail and waited for Gro to join her. There was plenty of room for two people to descend side-by-side, and Freya hated having someone behind her, an invisible presence constantly threatening to stumble and send her sprawling.

"Do you want something to eat?" Gro asked, attaching her own ropes to the right-hand rail.

"No." Freya never brought food of her own on these trips; the idea of eating on the platforms, let alone the stairs, made her uneasy. Anything that needlessly distracted her, lowered her guard or occupied her hands, could be dangerous. And whether or not that fear was justified, it was more than enough to guarantee poor digestion.

Gro reached back and managed to pull a small loaf out of her pack without unstrapping it, then started chewing as they began their descent. "Here's a hypothetical to ponder," she said, her words muffled by the contents of her mouth. "If a dozen new geysers appeared tomorrow, what would you do? Walk away from all this, or keep going?"

Freya wasn't sure that her own choice would really matter, now. "Wouldn't it make more sense to ask one of the youngsters?"

Gro didn't dispute that, but she'd already decided to have her say. "If it were up to me, I'd keep going."

"Really?"

"The geysers will always come and go; we could never be sure we wouldn't face the same problem again. And having come this far, we'd be foolish to waste it—to throw away all that expertise, in the hope that we could start again from nothing if we had to."

"Hmm." Freya was inclined to agree, though she doubted that the farmers would be willing to keep feeding them. "You haven't heard rumors, have you?" If there'd been an eruption nearby, half the farmers in the area would already have departed to stake their claims over the fresh soil. But if a geyser had appeared on the other side of the world, with no hope of any of the locals benefiting, word of it would come far more slowly, and take much longer to be confirmed.

"No, I'm just thinking out loud."

In the silence that followed, Freya's thoughts drifted, only to settle on her unnatural surroundings. The stairs were set deeply enough in the slanted column that she suffered no fear of toppling sideways, even if that offered the most direct route to death: if she somehow ended up on the cylindrical surface, she would rapidly slide around it, plummet through the air, and crash into the plain below. But it was the unobstructed descent ahead of her that always seemed most perilous, beckoning her forward, inviting her to trip and fall. And however confident she was, intellectually, that any such fall would drag her no farther than the next supporting post for the safety rail, some part of her mind refused to accept that: the slender ropes from her wrist to the rail felt like ineffectual talismans, utterly useless against the power of the stairway's vertiginous gradient.

Everything about the construction so far was a triumph of fact over intuition. She still couldn't stare at the slanted tripod legs without expecting them to topple over. The counterweights that rose vertically from each foot, lessening the risk that the torque would tear the base from the ground, just looked like a joke, a gesture, as manifestly inadequate as the ropes. She wouldn't be happy until the columns actually met up, visibly supporting each other. But then the whole construction would need to be repeated for the next level, even more precariously, with the legs of the new, wider tripods rising up from the tops of the old ones.

"Do you think we'll live to see the second level complete?" she asked Gro.

"We might. If the Yggdrasil keeps pumping the same amount of water in total, those columns should rise three times faster."

As noon approached, they were still only halfway down the stairs. They stopped to rest, waiting out the darkness as the sun disappeared behind Tvíburi. Against the backdrop of stars, the black disk of their twin softened to a bluish gray, lit by the half of their own world that was not yet in shadow, glowing in the Tvíburian midnight sky.

WHEN THEY REACHED the ground, Erna was waiting for them.

"There's been a fall," she said.

Freya nodded grimly, sickened but unsurprised. She'd heard that some of the younger workers had stopped using safety ropes on the stairs, and apparently all her warnings had come to nothing; some people were just too impatient to care. "Who is it? Is she in the medical tent?" Freya started walking toward the tent, trying to control her anger. Reprimands could wait; the poor woman would be suffering enough from her bruises.

"It's Sonja," Erna replied, hurrying after her. "They've taken her to the tent, but…"

"But what?"

"She's dead, Freya."

Freya stopped. "How can she be dead?" No one had mentioned any accidents before she ascended that morning for the inspection. "How long were they treating her?"

"She died when she hit the ground. She fell straight down, from the very top."

"Not down the stairs? She fell from a platform?"

Gro had caught up with them. "How?"

Erna said, "I don't know. You'll need to talk to the people who were up there with her. But we're still waiting for them to arrive."

The body lay on a stretcher on the floor of the medical tent, covered by a tarpaulin. Freya lifted one corner, then replaced it.

"Do you know if her mother's still alive?" she asked Gro.

"She is."

"I'll need to go to the village and tell her."

"Of course," Gro replied. "But I think you should wait until we have some idea what happened."

Freya covered her eyes with her forearm. Maybe it had just been a matter of time, but they'd come a long way without a single death. She'd always imagined that if it did happen, it would be part of a calamity that ended the whole project—some miscalculation that saw a whole column of ice snap at the base and crash to the ground. And though she could see why some people resented the encumbrance of the safety ropes on the stairs—where a tumble would be brutal but might well be survivable—surely everyone's natural instincts compelled them to take infinitely more care around the edges of the platforms.

She turned to Erna. "Which tripod was it?"

"The northernmost."

"When should the witnesses be down?"

"Soon."

"I'm going to go wait for them."

The three of them trudged over the ice, huddled against the biting wind. Maybe the whole thing had been the purest kind of accident, with a gust of wind knocking Sonja off the platform as she switched her second safety rope to a new anchor, and by chance the first one frayed, or its point of attachment came loose. The air was thinner up there, but the wind was faster; it could take you by surprise.

"Which leg?" Freya asked, as they approached the northern tripod.

"I'm not sure," Erna admitted.

Freya's anger returned; every ascent was supposed to be logged in detail. "Do we even know who was up there with her?"

"Lofn, Juliet, and…your niece."

Gersemi. Freya felt a pang of shame, as if this compounded her own culpability. But she had never been softer on Gersemi than she had on anyone else. And apparently it made no difference anyway; they all ignored her pleas to take the protocols seriously.

When they reached the nearest leg of the tripod, Freya peered up along the staircase, but she couldn't see anyone descending. She wasn't going to run back and forth between the three legs, waiting for someone to come into view; she sat down on the staircase and motioned to the others to join her. At least here they were sheltered a little from the wind.

Gro said, "They must have been fitting the last sets of double doors."

That made sense, but Freya still wondered about the timing. "Then they were well ahead of schedule." She and Gro had only just started their inspections; it would be days before they reached this tripod. And in any case, she never put pressure on anyone to rush their work. It was the ice that set the pace in the end; they wouldn't get to Tvíburi a day sooner by hurrying some bit of carpentry.

Freya heard footsteps from above. She turned and looked up, then rose to her feet and walked away to get a better view, but she could still only see one person descending—bounding down the stairs with the kind of urgency that made Freya wonder bitterly if this woman thought there was still a chance that she could help her friend.

"I think that's Lofn," Erna said.

"So where are the others?" Gro asked.

Freya almost replied, *Taking their time and using the ropes, because they've finally learned their lesson.* But she had to get her anger under control; it was no more helpful now than Lofn's haste.

Lofn slowed as she approached the ground, but Freya waited for her to step onto the ice before speaking.

"You must be in shock," she said. "You understand that Sonja's dead?"

"Yes." Lofn couldn't look her in the eye.

"Is anyone else hurt?" Freya asked, as gently as she could.

"I don't think so. They're coming down the other way." Lofn gestured to the north, toward another of the tripod's legs.

Freya was surprised. "You weren't all together up there?"

"Two of us were, at the start," Lofn replied, staring at the ground. "Then we started crossing over."

"Crossing over?" Freya's puzzlement didn't last long: there was really only one thing the words could mean. "And that's how Sonja fell? Crossing over?"

"Yes."

Freya stepped forward and embraced Lofn, as much to control herself as to try to comfort the woman. Screaming questions at her while she was standing in the wind, shivering with grief, would be unspeakably cruel.

Juliet and Gersemi approached. Gro walked over and met them, speaking with them quietly. Juliet started sobbing.

Freya was tired. "Let's get out of the wind," she said.

IN THE EVENING, the whole crew assembled in the dining tent to remember Sonja. Freya hadn't known her well, but she clutched at every anecdote and every kind word, trying to prepare herself to meet the woman's mother. *She helped her friend Carla through her illness. She found a way to make the worst of the vegetables the farmers sent us almost palatable.* Freya wasn't going to traipse into the woman's village, pushing the corpse ahead of her on a cart, only to blather on about Sonja's noble sacrifice that had brought them all closer to Tvíburi.

She waited until the morning to take Sonja's three colleagues aside. She sat them down in the planning tent, with a pile of work logs by her side.

"How long has this been happening?" she asked.

"About thirty days," Gersemi replied.

"So talk me through it. You throw ropes...?"

"Yes," Gersemi confirmed. "One person goes to the top of each leg of the tripod, and we throw ropes between the platforms to join them all up. Once they're secured, we can cross over."

"Along the ropes. Hand over hand?"

"Yes."

Freya said, "How could you imagine for a moment that that would be safe?"

Lofn said, "You want us to spend our whole lives reaching for Tvíburi—and at the same time, you want us to be so timid that we can't even cross fifty strides on a rope?"

Freya understood what she was saying, but the answer still didn't satisfy her. "There are risks that we won't be able to avoid. But this wasn't one of them. You should save your courage for the times when it's needed."

"And you should do the same with your rules," Gersemi replied.

Freya was stung. "Are you saying this is my fault? *For asking you to protect yourselves on the stairs?*"

"No." Gersemi was abashed, but she added, "No one's happy wasting their time on the stairs—and the safety ropes made that seem even more foolish. But I'm not making excuses for what happened to Sonja. If we wanted this, we should have done it openly. We rushed things, we cut corners, to keep the supervisors from finding out. That was our fault, and no one else's."

Freya sent them away and went to prepare the body. She bandaged the broken limbs as best she could, trying to bind them into some semblance of the natural shape that the woman's shattered bones were no longer able to impose.

As she wound the fabric around Sonja's leg, her forearm brushed against the dead woman's abdomen, and she felt it twitch. She dropped the bandage and stepped away, wondering if she should run and fetch the medic. But that was insane; Hanna would never have stopped treating Sonja if there'd been any chance that she was still alive.

Freya approached the body and spread her hand over the place she'd inadvertently touched. The flesh was cold and yielding; even a person who'd lost consciousness and gone days without breathing would not be like this. But after a moment, she felt the movement again. The muscles of the abdomen itself weren't contracting; rather, something was pushing against them. Sonja had not survived, but one of her brothers was clinging to life.

"Hanna!" Freya shouted. She wasn't sure where her friend was, but she was usually close to the tent. "Hanna!"

Hanna came running, then stopped, confused. "What is it?"

Freya explained. "That's impossible," Hanna declared. "I palpated and listened, five or six times." But she walked up to the body, and Freya stepped aside.

Hanna dug her fingers into Sonja's belly, and Freya saw her start in surprise. "I don't know how I missed it. Do you know anyone who could...?"

"I'll do it," Freya replied. One of her brothers had died a while ago, and the remaining pair had grown docile with age. They were sure to resent the newcomer, but they wouldn't have the strength to kill him.

"Are you sure?"

The only thing Freya was sure of was that she owed this to the family. She said, "We don't have time to look for someone else."

Hanna fetched a scalpel. Freya couldn't watch; she sat on one of the beds, facing away, trying not to interpret the sounds she was hearing.

After a while, Hanna said, "I'm sorry. He was too badly injured."

Freya was numb. "I can't take her back to the village like that."

"I know. I'll stitch her up."

Freya cradled her head in her hands and listened to Hanna moving around the tent, fetching what she'd need.

Hanna said, "Did you know she was using a pessary?"

"No."

"That's why I missed the signs: there weren't any."

"Well, no one wants to have children out here." The herbs were meant to render a woman's brothers quieter, but Freya had never felt the need to take such intrusive measures herself. She was about to ask why the pessary had suddenly stopped working and let the surviving brother wake, but then decided that she really didn't want to hear a detailed account of post mortem changes in the womb.

"She didn't get it from me," Hanna said. "And it looks stronger than anything I would have supplied. A dose that high risks losing your chance to have nieces."

"Why would anyone do that?" Freya turned to face her; thankfully, Hanna's task was almost finished.

"When your brothers fall into the deepest sleep," Hanna explained, "it's easier to do certain things. Working at heights, for example."

Freya was confused. "Why? You mean some women lose their balance if there's a brawl?"

Hanna laughed curtly. "Not that I've heard. It's subtler than that. You know they share our blood supply? Just as an unborn child does."

"Yes."

"Well, they don't just take from it, they put back as well. And what they feed us can make us more cautious...or at least, that's the case when they're fully alert."

Freya had heard something like that when she was a child, but she'd thought it was just a folk superstition.

"Are you serious?"

"I've seen the difference it makes," Hanna insisted.

"But why would it work like that?"

"If your survival depended entirely on your sister's, wouldn't you want to do everything you could to discourage her from killing you both?"

Freya said, "Yes—but I expect she'd already be quite keen on staying alive herself."

"Of course." Hanna looped the needle through one last time, made a knot, then cut the thread. "But she'd also be capable of taking into account considerations to which her brothers were entirely oblivious. Do any of our brothers know what's happened with the geysers? Why we're building the tower? What's at stake here?"

"So you think some of the women have started silencing their brothers' qualms? They know that what we're doing is worth the risk—and they want that to be enough to keep them going."

"I think they want a fairer fight," Hanna replied. "They want to conquer their own fears, one against one—instead of four against one, with three adversaries who can't be reasoned with at all."

∞

FREYA WENT TO find Gro, to tell her that she was leaving for the village.

"Have you decided on a punishment?" Gro asked.

"I'm not going to punish them," Freya replied. "They know what they did wrong. Now we need to find a way to make it safe."

Gro was bemused. "The tripods will meet up soon, and the temptation will be gone. Why not banish anyone who tries the same stunt again, and leave it at that?"

Freya said, "The first level of tripods will meet up soon, but what about the next one? And the next? Do you think people will climb up and down all those stairs, just because we asked them to, long after we're dead?"

"Maybe not," Gro conceded.

"This thing isn't ours anymore." Freya laughed. "If it ever was. All we can leave behind is what we've learned: about the strength of ice, about the way the roots grow, about gravity, torques and forces. The rest is in other people's hands, and the ones who'll matter most haven't even been born yet."

She returned to the medical tent with a cart, then set off across the ice.

PART TWO

5 ~~~~~

LEANDER was not the brightest star in the sky, but it was the brightest that ever crossed behind Tvíburi. Rosalind set up the telescope to track it, lit a lamp and prepared the comparator.

She had chosen a night when the timing would be as close to perfect as the various celestial constraints allowed. Leander needed to approach Tvíburi's dark side, which meant the occultation had to take place well before midnight, when the sunlit portion of the twin was still skewed to the west. But then it was a question of balancing that requirement with the need to ensure that the sky was equally dark for both measurements: the one just before the occultation, and the one just before Leander set. Some of her friends had argued that it wasn't strictly necessary to do both on the same night, but Rosalind found the idea of a prolonged delay troubling. She was confident that she could trim and fuel a lamp in such a way that it would give out constant illumination from dusk to dawn, but keeping it burning longer, let alone extinguishing and reigniting it, would be inviting inconsistency. If she ended up dead, it wasn't going to be for a foolish reason like that.

Well before the occultation, she stopped down the light from the lamp and adjusted the comparator's iris until the switch back and forth between starlight and lamplight induced no perceptible change in brightness. Simply staring at Leander and assigning a number to the strength of its light would have been a hopeless task, but the comparator made even the slightest difference from the reference source jump out at her. She wrote down the current size of the iris; it told her nothing on its own, but if the same setting worked again halfway to the second measurement, that would reassure her that the lamp's output had remaining steady.

When she stepped away from the instruments to stretch her neck, she took care to shield her eyes from the light of Tvíburi, lest they lose their sensitivity. She didn't need to watch the two bodies drawing nearer in the sky; with Joanna's help, she'd calculated all the angles in advance and etched the landmarks she needed to be aware of into the wheel that turned the scope.

The night was cold, but there were tents around her on three sides, sparing her from the north wind. The tents hid the base of the tower, but she could see starlight glinting off the slender spike that rose up from the final tripod. She hunted for a softer, internal glow of lamplight showing through the ice, but it was late, and all her friends were probably asleep. That made her feel a little hard-done by, as if they'd owed it to her to keep a vigil, but she was the one who'd rebuffed their offers to join her on the ground for the measurements themselves. She hadn't wanted the distraction.

Rosalind returned to the telescope, and nudged it along its preset arc until Leander was centered in the view again. She flipped to the lamp and back a few times, to reassure herself that nothing about the setup had drifted unexpectedly, but any change that had occurred was subtler than her powers of discernment. She stroked the edge of the wheel gently with her thumb, gauging the time that remained. It was strange: she'd been less anxious than this before most of her jumps, even those from untried heights. Maybe the risk here wasn't as great as she was telling herself; if she made a mistake, one of her friends was sure to pick it up when they repeated the whole procedure. But to be complacent would still be foolish.

As she followed Leander along its path, the unlit eastern limb of Tvíburi crept into view, a bland, almost featureless gray against the deeper darkness speckled with stars. The contrast made the sister world seem closer and more quotidian than ever: it was almost as if she'd just pointed the telescope at the edge of a building, or someone was holding their hand in front of the lens. Half a dozen faint stars dimmed and disappeared behind the twin's disk; Rosalind watched them carefully, building up a sense of the progression as it would apply to her target—trusting Joanna's mathematics, but prepared to salvage the situation if it turned out that she'd mis-transcribed the results, or if the wheel on the scope's mount had slipped.

The furrows on the wheel declared that the light from Leander had begun to graze the upper atmosphere of Tvíburi. Rosalind waited; she didn't expect a visible effect until the path cut deeper.

At the halfway mark any dimming was still impossible to detect in isolation, but when she switched to the lamp and back a few times, she found she had to shrink the iris slightly before the two points of light appeared equally bright again. As Leander moved closer to the edge of the disk, she forced herself to stop trying to spot changes by anything other than the official method—but there was an unmistakable blurring of the star's image, with the once-sharp point shimmering into a faintly trembling ellipse.

Moments before the occultation, Rosalind flicked the comparator, adjusted the iris, checked and rechecked. She had matched the lights again, perfectly, she was sure of it—and then Leander vanished from sight.

She lay back on the viewing bench, drained but elated. "Half done," she muttered. Now all she had to do was measure the effect when the light from the same star took the longest possible path through her own world's atmosphere—and then she'd finally know whether the most dangerous moment in her life was one she'd already lived through, or whether there was greater danger still to come.

"I'LL RACE YOU to the next level," Joanna said, tensing her body in preparation to start bounding up the stairs.

Rosalind groaned. "Not today. If you're bored, feel free to run ahead of me, but I just want to conserve my strength."

"But we're almost there!" Joanna remained beside her, keeping step with Rosalind's measured ascent, but she was fidgeting impatiently as she spoke. "The sooner we arrive, the more daylight will be left."

Rosalind didn't reply; she had no intention of increasing her pace. Before a jump, she needed to be calm and unhurried. If she sprinted up the stairs, she might gain the advantage of a little more time before nightfall, but it would come at the cost of finding herself standing on the ledge feeling as if she'd been chased there.

The sun had just come out from behind Tvíburi, and it was still so high that its light had to travel obliquely through the wall of ice around them, bringing a diffuse, bluish glow to the western half of the spiral staircase. As she emerged from the shadow of the central column into the soft blue light, Rosalind contemplated the roots embedded in the ice, most visible as backlit silhouettes, but breaking through the wall in places to sprout the flowers that kept the air replenished. The Yggdrasil had served them well, but they had deceived it horribly. If she'd been alive at the time the tower was begun, she would have bet anyone that the tree would get wise and stop cooperating, long before its roots had accreted a spike of ice stretching halfway to Tvíburi.

"Can you imagine never having to climb stairs again?" Joanna asked. She made the prospect sound surreal.

"You don't think we'll be raising a tower of our own?" Rosalind teased her.

"Someone else can do that job."

"Really? Who exactly are you volunteering?"

Joanna said, "The children. I'll farm the crops, they can farm the ice."

"Why not?" They all had their own peculiar fantasies as to how the new life would be—and there was no point cautioning anyone not to get ahead of themselves. However solid its foundations, the tower itself had only kept rising through the sheer force of its creators' endlessly malleable hopes.

By mid-afternoon, a section of the wall had grown so bright that Rosalind was left half-blinded by its lingering afterimage each time she walked into the column's shadow. The stairs were meant to be uniform, and she ought to have been able to climb them with her eyes closed by now, but though she knew roughly where the dozen or so mistakes were in every flight, she didn't have the kind of flawless memory that would allow her to anticipate exactly when her ascending foot would need to land a little higher, or lower, or farther ahead. In any case, the occasional risk of a mis-step did nothing to make the journey less monotonous. The best thing about this trip was that she wouldn't be taking the stairs back down.

"You have to promise that you won't follow me," she told Joanna sternly.

"I don't even have my glider!" Joanna protested. "I'm just here for moral support."

"I wouldn't put it past you to have something hidden up there."

"Only food," Joanna replied. "But who doesn't keep a few seeds stashed on every level?"

"What kind?" Rosalind wondered. She hadn't eaten at all when they'd rested at noon.

"None of your business! You're meant to be flying light!"

"A handful of seeds won't kill me."

"I vomited in midair once," Joanna confessed. "It might not have been fatal, but it was certainly distracting. So don't expect any last minute snacks from me."

Rosalind started laughing.

"What's so funny?" Joanna demanded.

"I've vomited a lot more than once." How was it that nobody knew that the team's most experienced flier had heaved up the contents of her stomach—however meager it was—at least as often as she'd managed to keep it down?

⚭

"AT LAST!" JOANNA pressed her hand gratefully against the sign on the wall promising the end of level thirty-six, then raced ahead and disappeared around the curve of the staircase. Rosalind felt a twinge of impatience herself, but maintained her pace; if she was going to break a leg today, she'd rather save that for a more appropriate moment.

As she stepped onto the landing, she saw Joanna waiting by the exit. "You don't have to come out with me," she said.

Joanna scowled. "I didn't climb all this way to stay inside."

Rosalind hesitated. "What happened to your stash? Have you eaten it already?"

"No, it's..." Joanna gestured toward the connecting chambers for level thirty-seven; the pressure difference wasn't much, but it would still take time to go through and back. "I'll wait until you're done here."

"All right." Rosalind walked over to the exit and opened the first door; when she closed it behind her she was in total darkness. She squatted down and started checking the seal, probing it with her finger from bottom to top. A speck of grit had become caught in the strip, so she opened the door again and brushed it away, then repeated the procedure.

There were six doors in total. The seals were good, but they couldn't be perfect, and in combination they probably ended up leaking air at about the rate the root flowers were replenishing it.

Rosalind emerged from the darkness of the final chamber into dazzling sunshine. It was late afternoon, but out on the balcony the light was much stronger than down on the ground. Her skin tingled oddly in the rarefied air, and she could feel the rigid muscles closing off her windpipe, more efficiently than any of the door seals. She'd taken her last breath for a while.

She put her pack on the floor and slid the panels out, then set to work assembling her glider. Every individual panel had probably been replaced four or five times, and the bracing rods and runners even more often, but she still thought of it as the same one she'd used for her first serious jump.

Joanna stepped through the door, squinting at the sunlight. They nodded to each other, then Joanna approached and clasped her friend's shoulder. Rosalind squeezed her hand reassuringly: this had to be done, and it would be over soon enough. But it was a cruel irony that the cost of being here meant that Joanna would be the last to know the outcome, when all their other friends were already waiting at the base of the tower to greet the returning flier.

Rosalind finished putting the glider together, then spent twice as long checking it. One of the rods felt stiff; she pulled it out and replaced it with a spare. After that, when she pushed against the frame it responded like a single object, precisely as supple and as strong as she needed it to be.

She propped the glider up against the wall of the tower, turned her back to it, and strapped herself in, securing the belt around her waist.

All this time, she'd been so far from the edge of the balcony that the ground had remained out of sight. As she walked forward, the horizon took longer than she expected to appear: it was even farther below her eye-line than the last time. She was afraid to look up at Tvíburi, to compare the angles the two worlds subtended, as if that might drive the point home far more ruthlessly. She was still a long way from the top of the tower, but some kind of dream-logic tugged at her mind, whispering that if she wasn't careful, she might end up falling *toward the wrong world.*

Or rather, the right one, sooner than intended.

Rosalind turned back and raised a hand to Joanna, who reciprocated, smiling. It had taken a lot of courage for her friend to be here beside her, and a lot of strength to make it seem that it had taken none at all. Rosalind was glad that they couldn't speak now; there were no words for a moment like this. She reached up and grasped the glider's handle bars firmly, then turned away and walked quickly through the opening in the balcony, onto the ledge, and into the sky.

For a moment she descended almost vertically, but then the airflow grew strong enough to tip the glider, and she was facing straight down. Her body continued to harangue her for the unforgivable thing she'd just done, jangling her nerves like a terrified mother screaming at a child caught in an act of suicidal folly, even as the elation induced by the inexplicable lack of a timely impact and agonizing injuries did its best to argue its own case. Both responses were premature—and as the fall stretched on and on, with neither pain nor safety arriving to settle the argument, Rosalind's instincts began to cede ground to her more considered judgment. Which was a cautious *so far, so good.*

Below her, patchy red clouds floated above the ice field. The tug of the air on the glider was still weak, and through the handle bars she could feel how little the frame was stressed. It was hard to think of that as anything negative: how kind of the atmosphere to treat her so gently. But sparing her deceleration now could only have two outcomes: a rougher ride when the deeper atmosphere fought to bring her back to terminal velocity…or an even rougher end, if it failed to slow her sufficiently before the ground completed the job.

So be it. This was what the light of Leander had demanded of her. Tvíbura's atmosphere was much thinner than Tvíburi's, so the fall that would demonstrate whether or not the gliders could land them safely on the twin world, if they dropped all the way from the halfway point, could start from a much lower altitude here to compensate for that disadvantage. If her measurements and calculations were correct, a jump from the top of level thirty-six would be precisely as dangerous as the crossing itself.

As Rosalind fell past the clouds, the glider began to shudder, and then roll. She shifted her weight, trying to keep it level; it wasn't tipping very far, but it was lurching back and forth at an alarming rate. Her own skin was oblivious to the turbulence; all she could feel was a pressure and a chill that barely touched her, as if she were lying face down on a slab of ice, but wearing enough clothing to insulate her from most of its effects.

She surveyed the ground below, hunting for familiar features to note their scale and rate of growth, trying to judge her height and speed against the last jump. She spotted a jagged ravine in the ice, farther to her left than she was used to; had some chance wind pushed her to the east, or had the ground itself, whirling around the midpoint between the worlds, out-paced her own lateral velocity, diminished by altitude?

A cluster of low gray hills rose up on her right, ancient rock that must have been fresh soil a million generations ago. A patch of whorled ridges appeared in the ice below her, raked by the low sunlight. Whatever her rate of descent, it was clear now that she was traveling faster over the land than last time. That did make some sense: the glider bluntly opposed her fall, but eased the air aside as she moved forward. And if it had diverted a greater portion than usual of the energy she'd gained into horizontal motion, that might spare her some of the force of impact.

The glider's rocking grew more violent. Rosalind could feel one of the bracing rods bowing and relaxing under the onslaught. Sustained pressure was one thing, but this repeated flexing was uncomfortably close to her own action when she was trying to snap a thick twig. She wondered if she should risk letting go of one of the handle bars in order to take hold of the threatened rod; after all, she still had the straps around her waist. But then the glider lurched suddenly, sharpening her sense of how dangerously contorted her body might end up if she left even one hand free.

She could hear the rod squeaking now, the high pitch of its complaint cutting through the noise of the wind. The thickening air buffeted the glider with a relentless, random vigor, as if trying to fold and unfold it along every possible line of weakness, never persisting with the same attack for long, but never failing to return to it later.

She coughed to open her throat and inhaled deeply, but even as she was savoring the sweetness of the air and the rush of strength to her limbs, the rod snapped, leaving its two halves dangling uselessly from their connecting points. The glider deformed, with two panels pushing inward just right of her head, then everting again under the force of the wind.

She gazed down at the shuddering blur of the ice field, trying to take comfort from its proximity even as the speed of her descent drained that consolation away. The glider's frame was twisting, losing symmetry under its new regime, and the wind was both amplifying and exploiting the result. As the glider rolled and pitched, every sudden shift of orientation imposed its own new stresses, distorting the frame a little more.

And the angles were growing larger, the tilts more precipitous. If the glider overturned, it would break apart completely. She'd somersault with the debris for a while before it was scattered by the wind and she was left tumbling through thin air.

Rosalind tightened her left-hand grip, then reached down with her right hand and loosened the strap around her waist. As her body swung down, she reached up and snatched at the right handle bar, catching the end and then forcing her clenched fist rightward into a more secure hold.

She dangled from the handle bars, astonished equally by her own actions and the fact that they seemed to be helping. The glider was still rocking from side to side, but so long as she maintained her grip, she did not believe it would actually overbalance. *Wrist straps*, she thought, almost calm for a moment. The handle bars needed to be supplemented with wrist straps.

She glanced down at the ground, but struggled to interpret the faint pattern of blue-white streaks rushing by. There were no hills or ravines in sight now, and she was moving across the ice too rapidly to catch any of the finer details she was accustomed to using to gauge her height. Then she felt the sting of wind-borne dirt on her skin, and understood just how near she was.

She tucked her knees toward her head, and managed to force her feet onto the tops of the runners. The glider gleefully took the new distribution of weight as an excuse to start gyrating more wildly again, but before it could come close to overtipping, it slammed into the ice.

It bounced, twice, almost breaking her grip, spraying fine chips of ice onto her face as the runners scraped over the surface like paring knives. Rosalind kept her body rigid, certain that she alone was holding the frame together.

She tried to see where the glider was taking her, but one of the panels that had retained its position blocked her view. Abruptly, she was airborne again, tumbling, and when the glider struck the ice it was upside down. Rosalind felt an impossible tug on her right arm; she released the handle bar and let half of the glider tear itself away.

She lay still in the wreckage for a while, afraid that if she tried to move she would discover that she couldn't. Maybe the best thing would be to rest where she was, until the shock of the impact had passed. But what if she lost consciousness?

She rose to her feet and took a few tentative steps. One of her legs had been cut, but not deeply. She felt battered, and when she flexed her right hand she knew she'd broken a finger, but her back and her limbs were intact.

Rosalind looked up across the ice and saw the tower in front of her in the distance, glinting in the late afternoon sun. She knew where she was now, and how far she had to travel. It was going to be a long walk, but there was no chance of getting lost.

As she set off, she turned back to survey the fragments of the glider strewn over the ice. She was going to have to think of the next one as new.

"I'm convinced," she said softly. "We can survive the crossing." She marched toward the tower, repeating the words in her mind, hoping that she'd be able to speak them with conviction by the time she reached her friends. If she'd died, they would have had to go looking for another solution, but now there was no point believing anything else.

6 ~~~~~

AS she walked through the village toward her mother's house, Rosalind couldn't help but feel self-conscious at how well-fed she must have looked. Not everyone she passed was alarmingly emaciated, but no one was carrying any flesh in reserve. To be ashamed of the disparity would be foolish; there'd be no point sending the expedition to Tvíburi if they all starved to death waiting for their first harvest. And if the provisions and laborers the villagers had sacrificed to the tower for the last four generations had been a heavy price to pay, she wasn't exactly taking an easy path herself. Still, she could not recall the last time she'd really been hungry, and she doubted that was true of anyone else in sight.

When she entered the house, she saw that her mother had invited her paternal aunt, Marion, to the farewell meal, along with Marion's daughter, Celine. Rosalind embraced them all in turn, though she'd never been close to her father's side of the family.

They sat down at the table and began to eat.

"How quickly do you think the new villages will be established?" Marion asked. When Rosalind hesitated, she made the question more specific. "Do you think you'll be seeing Celine there?"

"I hope so." The older women had no expectation of reaching Tvíburi themselves. Rosalind turned to Celine. "If you ever have time, there's no harm in practicing with a glider. If you start from low jumps, it's not dangerous."

"Practice, and wait for the signal," Marion said.

Rosalind nodded. "By the time our children are old enough to help us in the fields, we should have sowed enough land for the farms to be visible through any decent telescope. Though I'll be happier still if I'm the one who looks up, to see a new geyser sprouting from the limb of Tvíbura. In which case, migrants will still be welcome...but we won't expect quite the same influx."

Celine laughed, but Rosalind's mother looked horrified. Rosalind offered her a questioning frown. *Would it be better if I wished an endless famine upon the world, just to make myself less lonely?*

Her mother said fervently, "Tvíburi is the future. We all know that. You're giving us a future we'd never have otherwise."

Rosalind was embarrassed. "I'll do my best," she said.

Mercifully, Celine was impervious to her aunt's solemnity. "How many stairs are there in the tower?" she asked. "From bottom to top?"

"I don't honestly know," Rosalind admitted. "If I tried to calculate the total now off the top of my head, I'd probably get it wrong."

"Don't worry," Celine replied. "When it's my turn, I'll make sure to count them, and I'll tell you next time we meet."

○○

THE LAST LEVEL of the tower was the tallest, and it had no stairs at all. Rope ladders stretched between the annular rest platforms, but though the bottoms of the platforms were helpfully painted red and the top surfaces blue, Rosalind struggled to perceive any fixed direction as up or down. She felt like an insect crawling along inside a hollowed-out tree branch, which a child had picked up and was whimsically turning this way and that. It was not that she feared being dislodged, and it seemed absurd to imagine that she could ever lose her way. But as she moved, hand over hand, in near weightlessness through the tube of luminous ice, the sense of disorientation was impossible to shake off. All she could do was embrace it, and hope she wouldn't throw up.

"Matilda told me it was beautiful up here, but I never imagined!" Joanna called out, from a dozen rungs behind her. Matilda had worked on completing the tower, when the only thing at the open end between the ice-farmers and the void had been a series of tarpaulins, which were meant to trap the air but were forever coming loose or getting torn. She'd once told Rosalind that she'd often had to spend half a day without breathing, while the tarps were repaired and air was pumped in from the level below.

Sigrid said, "I'll reserve the word *beautiful* for the first sight of fertile soil between my fingers." She glanced across at Rosalind from her adjacent ladder. "Or better yet, my first child born on that soil."

"Yeah, yeah," Joanna replied tetchily. "It's all about the practicalities; the rest is just a distraction."

"Do you think a thousand people should have died just to give you a pretty ice sculpture?" Sigrid retorted.

"No. But that doesn't stop me appreciating every part of what they built."

Rosalind knew better than to urge them to make peace, or even just spare her from having to listen to their nonsense. They'd never actually come to blows over these meaningless quibbles, so if they found the bickering helped them pass the time, who was she to object?

As their last day attached to their birth world wore on, the sun crept below them without actually setting, even as Tvíburi turned gibbous behind the wall of ice. Rosalind couldn't really discern its shape, but the slowly growing illumination from the west side of the ice ahead of her was all she needed in order to picture the new dawn sweeping over the face of the twin.

For all that the rules of light and geometry rendered everything she was seeing explicable, it remained deeply unsettling. If anything, what shocked her was that these strange sights made so much sense. As a child, she'd experimented with lamps and fruit, visualizing every stage of this journey. For the real sun, and the real worlds, to recapitulate her clumsy shadow play made her feel like someone half prophet, half puppet, unable to decide if she'd shaped this future, or if it had reached back in time and shaped her.

Then again, maybe light was just light, and spheres were just spheres, and the humblest piece of fruit cast its shadow no differently than the world itself.

When the sun finally went behind Tvíbura, leaving the softer glow of their destination to light the way, Rosalind counted the number of annular platforms she could make out above her—and for the first time, it had fallen from the usual eight all the way down to six. At first, she thought she might be losing a couple to the change in the light, but as she passed the nearest of the six, nothing emerged in the distance to make up for it.

"Almost there, almost there, almost there!" Joanna chanted excitedly.

"Do you think we're blind?" Sigrid replied irritably.

"No, I think you're entirely insensate."

Rosalind was beginning to suspect that the only thing that would keep them all from driving each other insane would be the prospect of making the farms big enough to start luring fresh blood from Tvíbura. The six expeditions would amount to forty-eight people in total, but they might not have much time to visit each other's villages. Only new migrants would swell the numbers in each one, and bring some semblance of normalcy.

As they approached the end of the ascent, even Joanna fell silent. Rosalind saw the five women who'd climbed ahead of her leave their ladders and enter the departure hut. And then she was in there beside them, clinging to a hand rail, watching Sigrid clamber over the edge of the entrance, then Joanna too. She looked around and everyone was there: Anya, Kate, Hildur, Sophie and Frida. She'd wanted someone to be missing, just so they'd have an excuse to climb back down and investigate the absence. But apparently everyone else had been relying on her to be the one who ducked aside and hid on a platform. Joanna should have done it; she was the last, the only one of them with a chance to act unseen.

"Are you all right?" Kate asked.

"Just a bit dizzy," Rosalind replied.

"Take a long, deep breath," Kate suggested.

Tower workers had been up here before them, carrying the supplies and preparing them for the drops, but since even the weather on Tvíburi might influence where each glider landed, it had been decided to dispatch both people and provisions as close together in time as possible. When her gaze fell on the exit, Rosalind felt naked without her glider at hand, but if everyone had done their job it would be waiting for her outside, already assembled.

People joked and embraced each other awkwardly in the weightlessness, exchanging their last words before Tvíburi. Anya went through the exit first; there was something comical about watching her carefully sealing in the air behind her, as if that mattered to any of them now. But it would only be a few days before the second expedition began their own ascent, so it would hardly be polite to deplete the pressure in the entire top level ahead of their arrival.

As the others followed Anya, Rosalind hung back. She'd spent most of her life preparing for this moment, and she believed that she and her friends had done everything possible to understand and lessen the risks. But if every jump she'd ever made might have killed her, none of them had induced the kind of dread she felt now. It clamped her hand around the rail beside her so tightly that she feared her injured finger would break again, while every other muscle in her body turned to mush. All this, even with her brothers comatose. *You have no idea how lucky you are*, she told them. If only she could have slept through the whole journey herself.

Sigrid entered the chamber; only Rosalind and Joanna remained in the hut.

"You first," Joanna insisted.

"Why?" There was usually no one more impatient.

"I don't know," Joanna admitted. "I just like the idea of being alone here for a while. Saying goodbye to the tower on my own."

"If you don't come through, you know we'll come and grab you," Rosalind joked.

"Only if you can catch me. If I jump down the center of the tower—"

"If you jump down the center of the tower, you'll fall so slowly that anyone crawling on the ladder could overtake you in no time. In fact, the ice-farmers probably miscalculated: I bet we're past the midpoint, and you'd actually fall upward."

Joanna smiled, and gestured at the exit. "Sigrid must be through by now."

Rosalind pulled herself over to the door, got it open and dragged herself into the chamber. Contorting in the darkness to check each seal, she lost all sense of the direction in which her legs had originally been pointing, until she realized she could recover it by thinking about the doors' hinges. When she finally emerged onto the balcony, she was the right way up—at least in Tvíburan terms.

She raised her eyes toward Tvíburi. She had never seen it clearly, unobstructed, from any other point on the tower, so all she had to judge this apparition against was the view from the ground. But if the swollen disk was duly magnified, it still did not look close enough to be welcoming. It was not at all like staring down at the ground, not even from her highest jump. It was just a circle of light in the void, and nothing in her instincts promised her that she wouldn't simply veer off course and vanish into the endless blackness around it.

Joanna touched her shoulder. Rosalind turned and leaned toward her, then pressed her forehead against her friend's. *I can do this*, she insisted to herself. What was the alternative? Crawling back down to the ground, mocking all the dead workers and starving farmers who'd given her the chance for a new life? Curling up in the void and drifting away to die?

Anya and Hildur had already started dispatching the supply gliders. Rosalind watched as the two of them maneuvered the next one onto the catapult. At some point, Joanna had argued that the members of the expedition would easily be strong enough to send themselves, and all the cargo they needed, plummeting into Tvíburi's embrace by muscle power alone—and no doubt that was true, but the consensus had been that a more consistent force was needed if they were to have any hope of arriving within a day's walk of each other, let alone the supplies.

The eight passenger gliders were tied to a rail at the far end of the balcony, and some of the other travelers were already making their inspections. Rosalind dragged herself over and joined them. She had no trouble identifying her glider; the style and materials were exactly the same as the one that had ended up in pieces on the ice field. She checked every rod and every seam, but whoever had put it together for her had done a good job. Matilda, probably. Rosalind would miss her, though hopefully not for long; Matilda had sworn she'd make the crossing herself at the first sign of greenery on Tvíburi.

Anya wound the catapult again, then she and Hildur fetched the last of the supply gliders. Each of the twelve crates being dropped contained a mixture of items, so that even if only one was recovered there would be no essential tools or provisions that were entirely absent. Rosalind did not believe for a moment that all twelve could be lost, unless they'd miscalculated some detail of the flight so badly that none of the more delicate, flesh-and-blood cargo would survive the journey either. But she still found herself hunting for a reason for her sense of apprehension. The air might be poisonous, the soil might be barren, the wildlife might be fierce and predatory...but those risks had been obvious from the first day Freya herself had suggested raising the tower. Rosalind was only afraid of the dangers no one had thought of before—and her chances of outguessing all her colleagues and predecessors at the last moment seemed slim. She had to reconcile herself to that, just as she'd accepted all the known risks. Just as she'd pictured her body a thousand times, torn apart as it skidded across the ice, she had to picture the eight of them, alive and healthy, gathered in their new village, wailing and screaming at each other that they'd been fools beyond measure for failing to prepare for, failing to bring, failing to imagine...the thing that she could not conceive of.

She closed her eyes. *There, it's done.*

She opened them just in time to see the last supply glider slide along the catapult and disappear into the void.

Rosalind grabbed hold of her glider and started dragging it toward the machine. There was no order of departure that they'd all agreed on in advance, but as the flier who'd tested every new altitude from the tower, she did not believe anyone would contest her right to go first, one more time. And she could not hang back, she could not go last. She was strong enough to be the first to die, if that was the fate they were all about to share, but the idea of standing on the balcony alone filled her with an unbearable sense of desolation. Let Joanna take that role, if it was what she wanted.

After Anya finished winding the catapult she helped position the glider, then she and Hildur held it still as Rosalind climbed in beside it and strapped herself in place. They had all rehearsed the procedure a dozen times, almost weightless, in a closed room three levels below. The only difference was that this time there would be no cushioned barrier to bring her to a gentle halt.

With the glider and the catapult blocking her view, Rosalind pictured the scene on the balcony, and judged the time. Too soon, and the act would seem abrupt and alarming, too late and people would start to worry that she'd lost her nerve.

But when the perfect moment came, she didn't hesitate, she just kicked the release lever. The catapult's response was too fast for her to analyze; she looked down past her feet and saw the tower below her, a needle of glinting ice that seemed to narrow down to nothing long before it touched the ground—and then even the top of it retreated into invisibility, leaving her with the gray disk of Tvíbura, and beyond its edge nothing but stars.

Above her, the nose of the glider limited her view, but she could see the world's shadow just beginning to encroach on Tvíburi's brightness. The progress of the eclipse would give her a sharper sense of time than the slower motion of the arcs of dawn and dusk; the shadow would come and go in slightly less than one seventh of a day, while her journey was predicted to take about one fifth. Until she hit the atmosphere, she would be part of the same majestic gravitational machinery as the twin worlds themselves, and unless the catapult had been egregiously misaligned or mis-calibrated, there would be no real uncertainty in her trajectory until the very end.

She was surprised at how calm she felt now. Once the tower had vanished, she'd had no cues to provide any sense of motion, and it would take a while yet for the tug of Tvíburi to add much to the catapult's initial impetus. She glanced back down, hopeful for a moment that she might catch a glimpse of whoever had followed her, though she knew that was absurd. If they'd wanted to cheer each other with their presence along the way, they should have contrived some kind of massive, blazing lamp that could burn in the void, turning each traveler into a beacon for the rest.

In the void, the stars were only a little brighter than on the ground, but they were impossibly sharp, and their colors far clearer. Rosalind found it strange that they were all so much bluer than the sun, when they were thought to be suns themselves, perhaps with worlds of their own. But who would ever know that for sure? No telescope could reveal it, and no traveler could endure the journey it would take to find the truth firsthand.

Her mind turned to her mother, but behind the ache of separation she could still find reasons to be content. No one would let her mother starve, and even if a majority of the young people began to leave Tvíbura, having fewer mouths to feed would help make up for the dwindling harvests. The village councils had had generations to plan for the transition, and her mother still had many friends who would be staying behind with her. Tvíbura would not become a wasteland or a graveyard—not in her lifetime, maybe never at all. Let her see her daughter's farm from afar before she died; that was all that Rosalind could hope to provide for her, but it would be no small thing.

BY THE TIME Tvíburi emerged from its twin's shadow into full daylight, proximity had changed everything. Rosalind had lain beneath the telescope, night after night, sketching maps of this terrain—committing as many features as she could to memory, preparing for the time when she'd lose the luxury of an all-encompassing view. But even those meticulous acts of cartography had never quite made the land real to her, and to see it now with her naked eyes in more detail than the telescope had ever revealed made her feel as if a story that she'd cherished and learned by heart, but never taken to be more than an entertaining myth, was suddenly bursting out from the pages of a book and wrapping itself around her.

The gray mountains were taller, and far more numerous than those of Tvíbura, which suggested that the geysers had always been more active, piling up insanely high deposits of soil fast enough to outpace erosion and allow their own weight, and the passage of time, to solidify them into rock. But even the flatlands rose up from the ice, high enough to prove that they were being constantly replenished. People had argued that if the soil here was the same as Tvíbura's, then the seeds that must surely have taken a ride on a geyser now and then would have left the twin world covered in grasslands, but Rosalind was not convinced. Even over the eons, the number of chances for a seed to have made the journey and land, undamaged, on anything but ice need not have been so great as to prove that the soil itself was inhospitable.

The storybook world expanded below her, with geysers and mountains retreating into the distance as the ice field commandeered the plot, preparing a thousand-page monologue detailing its every ridge and crack. Rosalind felt a prickling sensation on her skin. The glider itself was steady, but she could feel the panels growing warm around her back.

This was it: she was touching the atmosphere. And she was coming in fast enough for this rarefied upper layer to heat the glider, even before it delivered any perceptible force. She contemplated the gentle heat, refusing to let it alarm her. Joanna had taken her through the calculations: if every scrap of the difference in potential energy between the top of the tower and the surface of Tvíburi was used to raise the temperature of her body, the effect would be about the same as holding her hand a bit too close to a lamp for comfort. To be that hot for too long would be intolerable, then injurious, and eventually unsurvivable—but once there was any kind of wind to cool her, the actual heat she retained would start to fall short of that hypothetical limit. If she could have ensured that all the inflows and outflows of energy were averaged over the descent, she would have had a guarantee that she'd be fine. In reality, it would all be down to details of Tvíburi's atmosphere that no one had known how to measure in advance.

Rosalind fixed her gaze on the ice, picturing the chilly weather below as the heat shifted from cheerful to unpleasant. The glider began to tremble, then pitch; it oscillated unsteadily, then settled with its nose toward the horizon, leaving her facing straight down. A thin, hot breeze flowed over her body; somehow she'd expected the wind to be cool, as if the air's two roles were separable, and this merciful intervention would be like an independent bystander coming to her aid. But the truth was good enough: the balance was shifting, and as the hot wind blew more strongly, it also grew less fierce. As the air thickened, and slowed her more and more, it also had the capacity to absorb a greater share of the energy burden itself, and to carry more heat away.

Her view had shrunk to a region much smaller than any of her maps, but she'd retained a sense of the position of the landmarks that had gone out of sight, so she did not feel lost. As the ice field loomed toward her, she picked up lateral speed, flipping through the ever-expanding storybook, glossing over the details of the icy monologue, hoping to reach the end before dark. The air was merely warm now; she opened her throat and took a tentative breath. It was thicker than she'd expected, and carried a strange dusty aftertaste, but it seemed to satisfy her lungs. She waited a few moments, in case there was some delayed adverse reaction—as if her caution really mattered, when in the end she'd have no choice. But when she felt an unambiguous surge of energy spreading to her limbs, she inhaled again, deeply. The warmth and the strange smell made her cough, but the realization that Tvíburi seemed to be welcoming her filled her with equal parts elation, and shock at the stark reminder that the result could easily have been different.

The ice was a blur now, but the glider remained steady; Rosalind couldn't recall a flight as calm as this. The thicker air could only react more forcefully to her encroachment, but apparently its greater density also helped dampen out turbulence. If the glider broke apart, it wasn't going to do it in flight. Everything would depend on the landing.

The cool breeze she'd been longing for suddenly arrived, sending her clothes fluttering. She saw the glider's shadow racing over the ice, unable to outrun its pursuer, and she braced herself for the inevitable meeting.

The runners struck the ground, sliding forward at an impossible speed. Rosalind stared down at the ice, terrified that the frame would break apart while she was moving so fast that the abrasive surface would take all her skin off the instant she touched it. But if anything, the ride kept growing smoother. Maybe the runners had grown so hot that they were simply melting away the rough patches. But if the smallest obstacles could vanish, anything larger would still be fatal.

She kept her body rigid, gripping the handle bars tightly but prepared to reach out and grab one of the bracing rods if the glider deformed and the structure betrayed her.

The betrayal never came. Friction did its work, uninterrupted, and the glider came to a halt, intact.

Rosalind unstrapped herself and knelt on the ground, trembling. Then she crawled out from under the glider and surveyed her surroundings.

The ice field stretched almost as far as she could see in most directions, though if she squinted at the horizon she could make out one of the geysers she'd noticed from on high, and some hills to the north. Tvíburi's orbit had carried the whole world westward beneath her as she approached through the void, so she'd expected to land well east of the prime meridian; once she explored those hills, she could confirm exactly where she was.

The sun had moved a short way past Tvíbura, but every part of the home world that she could see was still in night. There was something comforting about the utter familiarity of the configuration; she could have looked up on any other afternoon and seen a near-identical sight. Nothing was back-to-front here, nothing was reversed or deranged, on its own terms. By day she saw Tvíbura's night, and her east was Tvíbura's west—but if two friends standing face-to-face could accommodate the meaning of left and right, the cartographic version should cause no greater confusion.

Something small and dark in the sky caught her attention. For a moment she wondered if it might be one of the gliders from the tower, but its motion was both too slow and too complicated.

As the thing came lower, she realized that it was a kind of lizard. But instead of holding its limbs outspread, stretching the membrane between them to act as a natural glider, it was moving them in a way that was making the membrane flutter. The action looked bizarre, and utterly counterproductive, but rather than sending the creature plummeting, these strange flutters seemed to be controlling its flight. And when it dropped toward her, instead of continuing to the ground—as every lizard she'd ever observed before would have been compelled to do—it rose up into the air again in a wide, helical trajectory, ascending so high that it disappeared from sight.

Rosalind began weeping with joy. Not only was the air here breathable, there were animals—strange, vigorous animals, who evidently suffered no lack of food. Whatever the absence of grasslands meant, this world had to be far from barren.

And they'd come with seeds, they'd come with tools, they'd come with generations of farmers' knowledge. All this time, Tvíburi had been waiting to feed her sister's children.

7 〜〜〜

BY sunset, five members of the expedition had joined Rosalind at the base of the hills. Anya had chanced on one of the supply drops along the way, and used the enclosed cart to drag the crate with her. The contents included blankets and a small tent, so they set up the tent and crowded in for the night.

There was no sign of Sigrid or Joanna, but Rosalind wasn't too worried yet. The protocol *"head for the nearest landmark to the north"* had sent six of them from the ice field to the same hills, but it was not a foolproof recipe for convergence—and when the six who'd met up so far had done their best to mark their own landing sites on a map, it had been clear that chance variations in atmospheric conditions had had as much of an effect on where people hit the ground as the timing of their departure and the systematic libration of the two worlds. It wouldn't be hard to guess the most likely places where the missing pair might have ended up, and if they followed the rules and waited to be found by a search party sent by the majority, everyone would be reunited before long.

Sleep proved impossible, but Rosalind resisted the temptation to walk out of the tent and start exploring. Many of the plans they'd made together before departing were sure to prove ill-conceived, but she wasn't going to start her new life with a frivolous rebellion against the sensible consensus that everyone should rest and regain their strength on the first night after the journey.

So she settled for exploring from her blanket: pondering the strange smell of the new world, the effort it took to breath the thicker air and the greater reward it offered, the unfamiliar insect chirps, the deeper tones of the wind.

∞

IN THE MIDDLE of the night, it started raining. No one had thought to set up a container to catch the ethane, so Rosalind went out and did it herself.

When she checked, around dawn, the container was almost three-quarters full—more than enough to keep them all healthy for days. She looked across the ice field and saw two figures in the distance, approaching slowly, arms around each other's shoulders.

She ran to meet them. Joanna was uninjured, but Sigrid had broken her foot.

"How bad is it?" Rosalind asked, stepping in to support her on the other side to Joanna as they continued on toward the camp.

"It'll heal," Sigrid insisted. "It's a clean break, it just needs a splint."

"All right." They had splints, bandages, and disinfecting ointments in every crate.

When Sigrid had been tended to, they left her in the tent to rest and began their sweep of the area to try to locate the remaining supply drops. Rosalind strode across the ice, diligently scanning the ground ahead for anything from an undamaged glider to the sparsest trail of debris, fighting the urge to keep looking up to check that it really was Tvíbura above her.

She was hungry, but that was more out of habit than need. The food they'd brought would have to be rationed carefully, with one meal every second day, but the air alone gave her a sense of vigor.

Around mid-morning, she found one of the supply drops. The glider was intact, apart from a small tear in one panel. She disassembled it and stacked the panels on top of the crate. As she started back toward the camp, she saw another of the flying lizards wheeling above her.

By noon, the travelers had recovered seven crates in total. By nightfall, eleven. They took a vote and decided unanimously to move on to the next stage of the plan; if they ended up desperately short of anything, they could always come back and search again for the twelfth crate.

But Rosalind was hoping that the glider in question had torn itself apart high above the ice field, leaving its cargo to plummet to the ground far short of all the other landing sites. Their luck could not be perfect, and if the cost of that was a broken foot for Sigrid and one missing box of supplies, that would leave her much less nervous than eight travelers entirely unscathed, twelve crates recovered, and some unknown price yet to be paid.

THE NEAREST SOIL deposit was about two days' walk north-west of the hills. They decided to send an advance party of four, traveling light, rather than lugging all of their supplies to a destination that might turn out to be unsuitable. Sigrid willingly forfeited her place, then the rest of them drew lots. Kate, Joanna, Rosalind and Anya picked the red tokens.

It was still early when they set out. As they skirted around the base of the hills, Rosalind found herself shooing away mites—or some kind of tiny black insect that fled from her approaching hand, but was too numerous for this discouragement to have much effect. Unlike the ones back home, none seemed to want to bite Tvíburans, but they were still curious enough to spend time exploring the foreigners' skin, and however many got the message that there was nothing palatable for them here, they clearly had no ability to share that knowledge with the rest of the swarm.

"What are they eating?" she wondered. She had yet to see anything that she recognized as vegetation.

"Each other?" Kate suggested.

"Very funny."

"There must be something growing up in the hills," Anya decided. "Some fungus that can draw nutrients out of the rock. Or maybe there are patches of soil that blew in and got trapped."

Joanna coughed, then burst out laughing.

"What?" Kate demanded.

"I think I just ate one of the insects." She probed the inside of her mouth with her tongue, then added, "Yeah, it went down, and it's not coming back. So if I'm still alive tomorrow, we'll know what we can use for food if we ever get desperate."

∞

THEY SET UP camp at nightfall, with their destination a smudge on the horizon. Rosalind was surprised that they'd spotted it so early; either they'd walked faster than she'd expected, or the mass of soil rose even higher above the ice than she'd estimated when she'd examined its shifting shadow through the telescope.

Halfway through the night, she woke to the sound of something pushing against the tent. She tried to clear her head, wondering if it might have been the wind. Then she heard it again. The fabric wasn't rustling in the breeze. It was being prodded.

The light of Tvíbura coming through the weave of the tent was bright enough to show her a small inward bulge in the wall, close to the ground, but this offered no real clues about the would-be intruder. Rosalind woke her companions, and took a knife from her pack.

She unlaced the entrance and stepped out. As she came around to the side of the tent, she saw a low, dark shape fleeing across the ice, moving with a rapid, elegant lope, heading north-west.

Joanna appeared beside her.

"Did you get a look?" she asked Rosalind.

"It wasn't very big. Maybe some kind of cat."

"Curious enough to give something strange and motionless a poke," Joanna mused, "but too shy to stick around when an animal of our size emerges. If they're the kind of neighbors we're going to have, I can live with that."

"Let's hope that it's our strangeness they're shy of," Rosalind replied. "Not a resemblance to something they've already learned to fear."

Their ancestors had hunted Tvíbura's predators to extinction, but that battle had relied on numbers and resources that could not be mustered at short notice here. Still, all they'd seen so far were a few lizards, aloof in the sky, some insects disinclined to bite them, and one timid cat. Rosalind lowered the knife, which she'd been holding up instinctively. One more day's walk, and they might at least discover what lay at the very bottom of the food chain.

AS THEY DREW nearer to their destination, it resolved into a high plateau. The hills where they'd met probably hadn't been much taller, but the color of this material was completely different: a rich brown, just like the most coveted soil back home. The gray of the hills here matched, almost exactly, the gray of the hills and mountains on Tvíbura, so why should other comparisons not hold? Rosalind couldn't explain why a giant mound of soil with no grass to bind it hadn't simply blown away, but she refused to believe that they were headed toward nothing but a useless slab of rock.

By mid-afternoon the wind was growing dustier, and the ice around them less pristine. Rosalind ran a finger over the ground then put it in her mouth; it tasted of soil. If she could breath Tvíburian air, belched up from Tvíburian oceans, what was to stop the geysers here from delivering soil that the plants of her home world could feed upon?

The closer they came to the plateau, the less it looked like desiccated, ancient rock. Kate said, "That's ripe for farming. I can smell it!"

Joanna broke into a run, and this time Rosalind joined her. They sprinted together over the brown muddy ice, shouting exuberant taunts at each other as they took turns gaining the lead.

When they'd almost reached their destination, Rosalind stopped and glanced back toward Kate and Anya, who were proceeding at their usual unhurried pace. She felt slightly foolish, but she didn't care. She had no more patience left.

She turned to examine the steep incline ahead. Where the approach to the plateau met the ice, the soil had spilled out and left a thin, loose coating, but once it started to rise it became pitted and clumpy, not at all like the side of a sandpile. She caught up with Joanna at the base of the slope.

"Are these some kind of roots?" Joanna wondered, squatting down to examine the tangle of pale, fibrous strands that poked out through the soil.

"That's what they look like," Rosalind agreed. "But the roots of what?"

They started up the slope, supporting each other, judging each step carefully as they negotiated the treacherously porous surface. The soil kept crumbling beneath their feet, but never catastrophically; their weight seemed to be collapsing a succession of small, air-filled spaces, but the roots were so tightly woven through the soil that it was impossible to start an avalanche.

When they came to an opening that might have been either a cavern formed by chance from a gap in the roots, or the mouth of a burrow dug by an animal, they skirted around it; this wasn't the time to start pestering the neighbors. The ascent was growing arduous, but Rosalind had no intention of resting or retreating. There was not much daylight remaining, and she did not trust the light of Tvíbura to reveal everything they needed to know.

Finally, they staggered up onto the top of the plateau. The surface ahead of them stretched into the distance, roughly level as far as Rosalind could see, but as she stepped gingerly forward it was clear that it was no smoother or less porous than the slope. She knelt down and probed the ground with her fingers. The "roots" were still tangled with the soil, but they seemed oblivious to their change of circumstance. There were no stems, or flowers, or leaves protruding from them into the air; in the distance, the ground looked lifeless, just as it had through the telescope from Tvíbura, but each time Rosalind took a few more steps and checked again, she found the same tough, pale filaments locking up the soil.

Joanna said, "So this is Tvíburi's natural vegetation? Its idea of grassland?"

"Apparently." Rosalind didn't think these strands could be something like Yggdrasil roots—part of an organism that drew its nourishment from below the ice, and which had merely trapped the soil by chance. This plant—or colony of plants— was living off the bounty that the geysers had rained down onto the ice, stabilizing it much as the grasses on Tvíbura would have done, but feeding so well on the soil itself that it had no real interest in sunlight.

"So how do we clear a field, out of this?" Joanna asked. "A scythe, a plow?"

Rosalind took the knife from her pack and knelt down again. There was so much soil here: enough for a thousand farms. And nothing to fight the crops for their view of the sky. But when she plunged her knife into the ground, it was impossible to move the blade sideways. The soil's existing tenants—invisible from a few strides away, let alone from across the void—were nonetheless so numerous, and so strong, that it was like trying to carve into solid rock.

8 〰〰〰

"**M**AYBE the other farmers are having more luck," Frida suggested. "If they've found better soil, or found some trick that we've missed to deal with the tanglers, they could be thriving already, while we're just wasting our time."

Rosalind looked around the tent. The last time the same idea had been raised, people had still been clinging to their pride: every group was meant to be self-sufficient, capable of creating their own foothold in the new world. But now she sensed that most of her colleagues were so despondent that they'd be willing to seek help anywhere.

"The soil itself is perfectly fine," Hildur insisted. "The seeds all germinate, before they're choked by the tanglers. If we could just transport enough soil away from the plateau, and set up a new, pristine field out on the ice, the crops could grow there, unmolested."

"And what's supposed to hold the soil in place, while we're waiting for the seedlings to spread their own roots?" Frida asked.

"We carve trenches into the ice," Hildur replied. "Deep enough to trap the soil, to shelter it from the wind. But once the crops become established, we can start smashing the walls between the trenches, one by one, until we end up with a continuous field."

Rosalind couldn't decide which part of this plan would take the most work: hacking up the ice to make the trenches, or filling them with soil when every handful had to be wrestled out from between the tanglers.

Anya said, "I think it's time to try everything. My vote would be to send a couple of people to tour all the other soil deposits in the region; there might be something we can learn from every one of them, whether or not there are people trying to farm them. But we should also start work on testing Hildur's idea."

Joanna said, "And what about my idea?"

Anya scowled. "If it kills you, we lose you and your brothers—"

"If it kills me, no one else needs to waste their time wondering about it." Joanna laughed softly. "I could easily have died in my glider—revealing nothing new or interesting about this world—and no one would have treated *that* as a calamity!"

Rosalind said, "When you ate the berries that the cats eat, you were sick for four days."

"That was worth knowing, wasn't it?"

"Only if you learn not to take the same risk again!"

Joanna sighed. "It wouldn't be *the same*. The tanglers *want* the cats to eat those berries, for whatever reason. They've made them nutritious for that particular animal, and they must get some kind of benefit in return. Maybe the cats travel far enough to excrete the seeds in places where the plant couldn't send them by any other means. But the cats don't eat the roots; nothing we've seen does that. And maybe if the parts the locals relish make us sick, the parts they avoid will have the opposite effect."

"There's no logic in that," Sigrid protested.

"I didn't claim it was a syllogism," Joanna replied. "But it's still a possibility, until someone tests it."

Anya said, "Let's have a break to think things over before the vote."

Rosalind was glad to get out of the tent; just standing beneath Tvíbura reminded her of how many supposedly impossible problems their predecessors had managed to solve. They could not come this far and fail. There was fertile soil all around her; all they needed to do was prize enough of it out of the tanglers' grasp. Hildur's proposal was daunting, but none of them were afraid of hard work. Rosalind tried to picture the expression on her mother's face when she saw the first farms rising up, not on the original soil deposits that had been mapped generations ago, but on their borders.

Joanna approached. "Are you going to vote for my plan?"

Rosalind laughed, exasperated. "What plan? I can still smell the vomit from when you tried the berries. What was your argument then? 'Look at how strong and healthy the cats are!'"

"It'll be a risk," Joanna admitted, "but it'd hardly be the biggest one we've taken. And it won't be easy to poison myself; those roots are tough. It'll take half a day to slice them up, and the rest to chew the pieces."

"Which is why we need to keep trying to grow actual food," Rosalind replied.

Joanna said, "None of these proposals are mutually exclusive. And believe me, I'd prefer to eat something that grows back home—though with turnips, honestly, would there be any difference? But we need to know exactly what we can and can't eat here, even if it's just a matter of having something to fall back on if there's a shortage of our own crops in the future."

Rosalind had no problem with planning for contingencies. It was the idea of making do with the tanglers that dismayed her.

"If we can't grow our own crops," she said, "how will anyone know that we survived? *How will they know that it's safe to follow us?*"

Joanna nodded grimly. "If the famine doesn't break, there'll be nothing more important than letting people know whether or not they can escape it here. But if we can find a way to feed ourselves without covering the soil with our own kind of crops, we'll just have to find another way to get a signal across the void."

Anya called them back in for the vote. In the end, everyone agreed to send emissaries in search of the other expeditions, and the vote was five-to-three in favor of testing Hildur's back-breaking plan.

But only Joanna voted for a trial of the tangler roots' culinary potential. Rosalind had tried to be objective about it, but she couldn't. She did not want to learn that there was a way to keep on living while everyone they'd left behind starved to death.

AS SUNSET APPROACHED and the other members of the team put down their picks and headed for the tent, Rosalind decided to keep working. She had almost come to the end of her second trench, and she wanted the satisfaction of finishing it before she slept.

Her shoulders ached, and she was famished, but each time she swung the pick, the spray of blue-white chips flying off the ice-face was all she needed as proof that she was making progress. This was how they'd finish the task: one strike at a time, over and over, until it was done. Tvíburi had made the job harder than it had to be, in ways she'd never expected, but their patience would wear the world down. Tvíburi would feed them, willing or not.

Her brothers squirmed and hissed, disturbed by her labors, but she knew they wouldn't grow any calmer when she stopped to rest. They'd woken from their long sleep more ardent than ever, and though she could hardly blame them for the expedition running out of pessaries, they ought to have been capable of noticing how poorly fed everyone was. Who tried to bring children into a world without crops?

"Rosalind? Is that you?"

Rosalind looked up to see a lone figure approaching across the ice. In the twilight, she couldn't make out the woman's face, but she knew the voices of her seven fellow villagers, and this wasn't one of them.

She put down her pick. "Your eyesight's better than mine," she called back.

The woman laughed, and strode forward to meet her.

"Erin?"

"Your eyes are still working." Erin removed her pack and they embraced.

"How's your group?" Rosalind asked. "Did everyone land safely?"

Erin looked down. "We lost Miranda."

"I'm sorry." Rosalind hadn't know Miranda well, and she decided not to reopen the wound with more questions.

"And yours?"

"We were lucky. Everyone survived."

Erin turned and surveyed the trenches. "I see you're trying the same thing as we did."

"You've done this too?"

"Yes." Erin hesitated, then added, "I should probably tell you about our experience."

"You'd be welcome to." Rosalind gestured toward the tent. "Come and rest, first. How long since you've eaten?" Erin looked remarkably healthy for someone who'd been walking for days, but it would still be impolite not to share what they had with her.

"Oh, I'm eating right now," Erin replied cheerfully, opening her mouth to expose a half-chewed, fibrous mass.

Rosalind was startled. "You're eating tanglers?"

"That's not what we called them, but yes. Just the roots. You do know the nodules are no good?"

She had to mean what Joanna had called berries, though they sprung from the tanglers' roots, and could only be plucked easily from the walls of an animal's burrow. Rosalind said, "That was made very clear."

Erin poked a finger into her mouth and dislodged the mass from around her teeth, shifting it to the other side.

"What else is your group eating?" Rosalind asked. The roots seemed to take so much effort to masticate that it was hard to believe the process didn't consume more energy than it yielded.

"Parts of the voles. The cats are too hard to catch. I know, the voles eat the nodules too, and some of their organs seem to concentrate the unpleasantness, but most of their flesh is fine."

Rosalind had more questions, but she led her guest toward the tent. "Frida and Joanna are off on a tour of their own," she said. "They might even have stumbled on your people by now."

"I have a map with all the villages on it," Erin replied. "Or I will have, once I add this place. So if you tell me which way they were going, I can tell you who they will have met first."

They entered the tent, and everyone embraced Erin. She refused all their offers of food, and the seven of them sat down in a ring on the blankets. They had no fuel for the lamps anymore, but there was enough light from Tvíbura to let them see each other's faces.

Once the pleasantries were out of the way, people started quizzing Erin about her village's agricultural experiments.

"We tried putting soil in furrows in the ice," she explained. "The first time, we did it close to the plateau, as you've done—to make the transport easier. But within six or seven days, there were...I think you call them 'tanglers'...growing in all the furrows. We assumed that the seeds must have blown in on the wind."

So much for our own efforts, Rosalind thought. But at least they'd now be spared wasting any more time on a flawed method. And she could feel the tension growing as people waited to hear about the next step: the one that actually worked.

"We repeated the whole thing much farther away," Erin continued. "We had guards watching, day and night, to shoo the cats away, in case they came and shat seeds into our precious soil. But the same thing happened. The tanglers appeared, just as quickly as before, and nothing of our own could grow."

"How is that possible?" Hildur protested. "Even if the wind is blowing the seeds far and wide, how could there be as many of them at a greater distance?"

"We must have brought them there ourselves," Erin replied. "The soil must be full of them, and they're either too small to discern, or too similar to the particles of soil to be picked out by inspection. Whatever the cats are spreading, it can't be the only means these things have of reproducing. We've tried washing the soil, sieving it through fabric, tossing it in the air and only using the parts that fall at different distances—hoping the wind will separate out the seeds and leave us with something we can use. But so far, whatever we do, we either end up with useless gray dust in which nothing at all will grow...or we end up with rich, brown soil full of tanglers."

9 ~~~~~

ROSALIND couldn't sleep, so she left the tent and walked out across the ice. It was close to midnight, with Tvíbura almost entirely in shadow.

She paced the encampment, repeating the calculations that had kept her awake, hoping she might have made an error that she could detect now that she was fully alert. But the results remained the same. Even if the people of all six villages devoted every waking moment to digging trenches in the ice and filling them with soil, it would take at least three generations to spell out an unambiguous message in letters large enough to be read through a telescope.

Maybe a written message wasn't necessary; any clearly artificial structure would demonstrate that the colonists were still alive. In the absence of recognizable farmland, that would still prove that there was a source of food here. But would anyone actually make the crossing from Tvíbura on no other evidence than a few baffling lines appearing in the ice? If they were desperate, if they were starving, maybe a handful of people would interpret the peculiar artefacts as signs of hope; maybe there would even be enough of them to support each other in all the tasks they'd need to perform to make the crossing safely. But it was hard to imagine an influx so great that it became self-sustaining, with the new arrivals so numerous as to add significantly to the artefacts' drawing power. Most people would need a clear promise that a better life awaited them on Tvíburi—and most people would find that unimaginable in the absence of the kind of plants they were accustomed to eating.

She heard a rustle of fabric, and turned to see Joanna emerging from the tent.

"Are you thinking what I'm thinking?" Joanna asked.

"Possibly, but tell me anyway."

"We need to do something with the root cuttings."

Rosalind took a moment to understand her meaning; most of the talk about "roots" that she'd heard lately had concerned the tanglers.

"Do what with them?" They'd brought the Yggdrasil cuttings with them on the chance that, if there was a local variety that lacked some of the qualities needed to grow a second tower, the two kinds might be spliced together. The idea itself wasn't entirely fanciful; farmers had sometimes succeeded with heterogeneous grafts for other kinds of plants. But there was no sign of any local version of the Yggdrasils at all.

Joanna said, "Drop them in a hole that takes them all the way down to the ocean."

"Into a geyser?" Rosalind was bemused. "Even assuming that they find the conditions amenable down there—with no competitors as brutal for them as the tanglers are for the crops—how long do you imagine it would take for the tree to get its roots up to the surface?"

"I don't know," Joanna confessed. "Generations, for sure. But that's no reason to put it off. If we don't do everything in our power to make it possible to get word back to Tvíbura, people are going to go mad. It's hard enough accepting that there's probably no way to achieve that in our lifetimes, but at least we have the tradition of the tower-builders to fall back on: if they could work for something that they knew they wouldn't live to see for themselves, we can do the same. It won't be enough to make anyone content, but it might be enough to keep us from losing hope."

Rosalind couldn't find much comfort in this definition of *hope*: some small chance of the cuttings thriving in the ocean; generations for the roots to break the surface, then generations more for a second tower to be grown. She wanted her friends to join her before she died. She wanted her mother to live long enough to know that the expedition had succeeded.

But she had no idea how to make those things happen.

"We don't seem to have any other use for the cuttings," she conceded, "and if half the villages keep theirs, just in case, I can't see any harm in trying."

"So you'll vote with me on this?"

"Yes." Rosalind stopped to ponder the practicalities. "Which geyser are we talking about?"

"The closest one to the closest point to Tvíbura," Joanna replied. "I don't care how far I have to walk, but if the Yggdrasil is to be of any use for tower-building, we need the roots to emerge in the right position."

"The terrain around there looked a bit tricky." Rosalind had found the strangely sculpted ice deposits quite beautiful when she'd been gazing down at them through the telescope, but she'd never contemplated trying to scramble over them.

Joanna didn't dispute this assessment. "So if you're coming with me," she said, "don't forget to pack plenty of rope."

∞

THE GEYSER ROSE highest around midnight and noon, dying away completely by sunset and dawn. Rosalind watched the white column ascend every morning, wondering if the glimmering haze contained a few droplets of water, or if the spray bursting out from the buried ocean froze entirely into powdered ice by the time it reached the surface. It was strange to think that the same eruptions had once been so common on Tvíbura that everyone in the world would have seen at least two or three in their lifetime, and many would have witnessed them up close. The marvel she was approaching had been entirely commonplace.

In the evenings, they often saw cats out on the ice, and by day, lizards overhead. No animal here was quite the same as anything back home, but they seemed too close to Tvíburan species to have no kinship with them at all. With plants it was another story, but perhaps the tanglers were the oldest, purest Tvíburians, and they'd conquered their territory long before any Tvíburan seed tried to gain a foothold. Rosalind could not imagine a cat being flung from world to world by any means and ending up alive, but if ancient lizards had flown in the skies of Tvíbura when its own air was thicker, it was not inconceivable that they could have survived the crossing.

By the fourth day of their journey, the geyser was beginning to resemble an ephemeral version of the tower: a white streak bisecting the horizon and stretching toward the zenith, tapering to invisibility long before it actually came to an end. There was a faint, low rumble in the ice that presaged its appearance, catching Rosalind's attention just in time for her to follow the top of the fountain as it rushed into the sky.

Though the column of ice-dust came and went, it rose from a permanent base. It was hard to discern when the geyser was flowing, but in the late afternoon, when the sun had moved on to squeeze the ocean out through other vents, a low, broad cone of ridged and jagged ice emerged from the haze.

On the morning of the sixth day, the hard, flat surface of the ice field, compressed by time and worn smooth by wind and dust, began to acquire a smattering of fragile encrustations, shaped more like delicate sculptures than anything that belonged to the realm of geology. Rosalind did her best to avoid them, but as they grew more common she grew impatient with the need to weave a complicated path around them, and started crunching them underfoot.

"Why don't they just lie flat?" Joanna asked, irritated but still curious. She squatted down to inspect one of the deposits. "You know these things are mostly thin air? They're like shrubs sprouting ever finer branches, taking up space without actually containing much ice. But I don't know what makes the ice from the geyser so special that it doesn't fall straight to the ground."

Rosalind pondered this. "The ice *dust* might fall straight to the ground, but if there's vapor it could condense around whatever's already there."

Before long, there was no unencrusted ground remaining; everywhere they trod, ice crumbled beneath their boots. And with each step, they found themselves sinking a little deeper, demolishing ever taller structures before their soles ended up on solid ice and they were left ankle-deep in the surrounding deposits. But then, even more disconcertingly, the lower portions of the ice-shrubs began to resist their weight—with the upper parts still collapsing, leaving them perched on the jagged remnants.

"How did people ever do this, back on Tvíbura?" Joanna wondered.

"What makes you think they were ever stupid enough to try?" The view from on high had been misleading; Rosalind had been prepared to face a craggy landscape built of solid ice, but no amount of rope was going to render this terrain traversable.

"I wouldn't call it stupid," Joanna protested. "How could you know there were cracks in the ice going all the way down to the ocean, and not want to take a look? And just because we're unprepared, it doesn't mean they were."

Rosalind could recall children's stories where people both innocent and wicked had been cast into the chasms by their antagonists. But those tales had been woefully light on detail about the method of approach.

Joanna cried out in pain, and spread her arms to stay balanced as she tried to take the weight off her right foot.

"How bad is it?" Rosalind asked.

"It stabbed through the sole of my boot, but I don't think it went far into my foot."

Rosalind pictured the two of them walking with Joanna's arm across her shoulder; anywhere else it would have been the right thing to do, but here it was only likely to make things worse.

Joanna raised her foot and brought it down again slowly, angled slightly.

"We need to get back on solid ground," Rosalind said.

"I'm not giving up!" Joanna replied angrily.

"I never said we should. But you need to put a bandage on that. And then we need to find a better route."

As they were retracing their steps, Rosalind heard the usual rumbling and felt the wind rising up, blowing toward her from the ice field. She turned to see the geyser ascending; they were so close now that the column of white haze blotted out a third of the sky. As she raised her eyes toward the vanishing point, it looked as if the torrent of ice dust was tumbling *down*, falling toward Tvíbura—as if their dying home was reasserting its power. But Tvíbura had nothing to do with it, and even the sun was cheating: squeezing the trapped, subterranean ocean, raising the pressure in one direction and lowering it another. Down was still down, and no quirk of gravity was going to lift her up off this accursed ground and drag her into the sky.

She looked down again and kept walking gingerly across the perilous surface. After a while, she felt an odd sensation on her skin; she inspected her palms, and saw a faint, branched pattern catch the light. The fine coating of ice cracked and splintered as she flexed her hands. She blinked, and felt the same thing happening on her eyelids.

CO

THEY SET UP camp out on the ice field, and Joanna rested her bandaged foot. "I don't know how long it's going to take us to learn to repair boots with anything Tvíburian," she lamented. "Did you see the fabric Hildur wove from tangler fibers? After one day wearing that I think it would take most of your skin off."

"We'll learn how to treat the fibers to make them softer," Rosalind asserted, trying to keep them both optimistic. "And we still haven't cataloged all the less common plants. Nobody made the plants on Tvíbura for our benefit; we just discovered ways to use them, over time. It will be the same here."

"Maybe."

The next morning, they left their tent standing and set off in a broad arc around their target, hoping that a combination of influences—the prevailing winds, the topography of the ice field, and the shape of the chasm itself—might direct the falling plume of ice dust and water vapor in such a manner that a path was left clear. But while the edge of the region plagued by encrustations moved closer to the chasm for a while, it soon reversed direction and forced them away again.

It took them all day to come full circle.

Joanna limped to a halt in front of the tent. "We need to come back with wooden boards we can put under our feet," she said. "Strapped to our boots, to spread the weight over a larger area."

Rosalind said nothing, but she suspected that that would just delay the inevitable: they might succeed in crossing more of the fragile ice before it gave way beneath them, but when it happened they would only plunge deeper into the pile of icy spears and blades that the geyser had been stacking up around itself since its inception.

She looked up wearily toward Tvíbura. A lizard was circling overhead; she'd seen so many of them close to the geyser that she was starting to wonder if there was some kind of oceanic insect that they were feeding on—snatching it out of the air as the geyser delivered it, stunned or dead, into this strange, hostile world that the poor creatures could never have imagined existing.

"I know how we can get the root cuttings into the chasm," she said.

"With my ice shoes," Joanna replied, puzzled, as if the matter had been settled.

"We saw some cliffs to the north," Rosalind reminded her. "Not much farther from the geyser than we are now."

"What has that got to do with anything?"

Rosalind said, "The ground's not safe to walk on, but the lizards have no trouble with the air here. I'll glide off the cliffs, and let the updraft carry me over the chasm."

10 〜〜〜

ROSALIND took her time, studying the lizards as closely as she could, contemplating the modifications she would need to make to her glider if she wanted to mimic the way they spiraled up around the geyser. Trying to create panels that undulated like the lizards' membranes would be absurd, but adding a system of struts and levers that allowed her to flex the whole shape slightly, giving it enough asymmetry to force it to swerve left or right, seemed like a reasonable ambition.

She made the changes, then carried her glider to the top of the plateau to test the new design. But as she ran toward the edge, her courage failed her. She stopped and knelt down on the tangler-infested soil, trembling in horror at the risk she'd almost taken. If anything had gone awry, she could have dashed her skull open on the ice below.

She left the glider where it was and made her way carefully down the slope, relieved to have abandoned the whole insanely reckless notion. It was only when she was back on level ground that she paused to reflect on the reasons for her change of heart.

Rosalind stood on the ice for a long time, weighing up her options. Then she went looking for Sigrid.

"I think it's time," she told Sigrid. "We know we can survive on the tanglers and the voles. We can feed and shelter ourselves. And we understand the animals here well enough not to fear them. Nothing's certain, but someone has to be first. And I know you'd make the best mother, out of all of us."

Sigrid was amused. "If your brothers are annoying you, just say so. You don't need to flatter me."

"But you agree?"

"Yes. When do you want to do this?"

"Tonight," Rosalind replied. "Up on the plateau, where we'll have some privacy."

As the time approached, Rosalind tried to keep her mind on other things. She spent the afternoon helping Hildur with her weaving, then she chatted with her fellow villagers, pursuing every idle topic that arose, prolonging each distraction for as long as she could.

"Are you all right?" Joanna asked her.

"I'm fine."

"How are your experiments with the glider going?"

Rosalind said, "There are some aspects that are proving trickier than I expected. But I think I can sort them out."

At sunset, she left the tent on the ice field and headed up the slope. There was a second tent, on the plateau, that had been largely abandoned since their farming experiments had failed. As Rosalind entered, Sigrid called out to her; she had followed close behind.

"Don't be nervous," Sigrid told her, as they knelt down together in the near darkness. "Before I joined the expedition, I let one of my brothers breed. It only seemed fair, before they faced the long sleep. And I can promise you, it's not that difficult. Just relax, and he'll know what to do."

They loosened their clothing and brought their bodies together. Rosalind felt all three of her brothers scrambling to take advantage of the opportunity, but the struggle didn't last long. The winner emerged, protruding from between her legs, crossing the narrow gap between the women, determined to father a child.

Sigrid gasped, but didn't flinch; she wrapped her arms around Rosalind to keep their bodies from being pushed apart. Rosalind listened carefully to her labored exhalations, trying to judge the progress of the act. She had no experience at all, but she'd heard enough talk from other women to know what to expect.

Sigrid shuddered, then relaxed. Rosalind pulled away from her as quickly as she could, then reached down and took hold of her retreating sibling before he could disappear. She got to her feet, hitching up her trousers with her other hand, and headed out of the tent.

"Are you all right?" Sigrid called after her.

"I'm fine," she replied. "It's just the pressure on my bladder..."

Rosalind walked carefully across the uneven soil, afraid of tripping on the tanglers. When she was far enough away from the tent, she knelt down on the ground and groped in her pocket for the knife.

Before her brother could sense what was happening and try to change her mind, she pushed the blade into his body and forced it through to the hilt. He squealed and thrashed, but the handle of the knife was jammed against her thighs, so the more he tried to retreat to safety, the more damage the blade wreaked.

When he stopped moving, Rosalind cut off everything that protruded and buried it in the soil. She was weeping softly, but she hardened her heart. He'd fulfilled his purpose; she'd given him that. She would do the same for the other two.

She had no choice. However repugnant this fratricide, she couldn't spare them. She had her purpose too.

ONCE ROSALIND HAD perfected her technique, she demonstrated her modified glider to the rest of the village: launching off the plateau, and completing a rough circle over the ice before landing.

Afterward, they gathered in the tent and she sketched out a plan that she hoped they'd find plausible.

"You'll start flying while the geyser's active?" Kate asked, troubled by the notion.

"It's the only way to get above the chasm," Rosalind explained. "I need a strong updraft. Even starting from the cliffs, if I tried to approach while the geyser was quiet, I'd just crash into the needle-ice before I was even close."

"So you approach, you circle around waiting for the geyser to stop, then you swoop over the chasm, drop the root cuttings... and hope you get back to solid ground before you lose altitude?"

"Exactly," Rosalind agreed. "But when you say 'hope' that makes it sound like a huge gamble. I'll make sure I'm high enough to start with so it won't be unlikely at all."

Kate looked dubious. "And when you say 'I'll make sure' that makes it sound as if you've done all this a thousand times before."

Rosalind said, "Either I try it at the real site now, or I give up. I've practiced as much as I can."

They voted in her favor, six to two, with only Kate and Frida unconvinced. Joanna would accompany her, since she knew the terrain already.

As they left the tent, Sigrid touched her shoulder and whispered, "Good news. Your brother should be happy."

Rosalind said, "We should all be happy."

"We will be," Sigrid assured her, "when we see the child born."

∞

WHEN THEY SET out for the geyser for the second time, Joanna was uncharacteristically subdued. Rosalind wasn't sure what was troubling her, but after a day walking in near silence, she tried to break the mood.

"Are you annoyed that no one went for your ice shoes?" she teased her.

"Not at all," Joanna replied. "I'm sure the glider's a better idea."

"I'll be careful," Rosalind promised. "I know how important this is."

They were halfway through raising the tent when Rosalind felt a cramp in her abdomen. She excused herself and walked away across the ice, getting as far as she could before the pain stopped her, then arranging her clothes to conceal as much as possible and hoping that it looked like she was defecating. She'd thought her body would expel the dead tissue swiftly, and when it didn't happen within a day or two she'd wondered if she'd somehow resorbed it. But now all three of the shrivelled roots came out, in a rapid succession of bloody convulsions.

She squatted on the ice, shivering, trying to compose herself. Whatever happened at the geyser, at least one child was coming. She'd have a niece to survive her; she had to take solace from that.

By the time she got back, Joanna had finished with the tent and was lying inside, feigning sleep. Maybe she knew about Sigrid, and Anya, and Sophie, and was hurt that Rosalind hadn't confided in her. But if they started talking about the subject at all, it might be impossible to stop.

"Sleep well," Rosalind whispered. She laced up the entrance and lay down on the blanket, hoping they wouldn't be disturbed by the cats.

∞

THEY VEERED NORTH as they approached the geyser, following a gently sloping route to the top of the cliffs. Rosalind kept seeing lizards circling the chasm, and if that in itself promised nothing, at least it was more encouraging than their absence would have been.

"Someone took an awful lot of ink from the stores, just before we left," Joanna said, apropos of nothing.

"Really?"

"You know how much I use, myself. So I couldn't help noticing what was missing."

Rosalind said, "We'll find a good substitute eventually. The right kind of plant resins, the right kind of minerals...people have just been busy with other things."

Ahead of them, the geyser erupted into the sky. Joanna stopped. "Do you want me beside you on the cliff, or do you want me to hang back?"

Rosalind didn't know how to answer that. Joanna walked up and embraced her. "You know it might not work?" she said. "I've tried to estimate the velocity, and I think it might be close, but it's hard to make the measurements precise."

"I know. But I need to try."

"Yeah."

Rosalind tightened her hold on her friend and imagined retreating, the two of them walking back to the village together. Then she released Joanna and stepped away. "You should stay here," she decided. "Just tell the others I got the cuttings in."

"All right."

Rosalind turned and walked up the slope toward the cliff. A dozen or so strides from the edge, she took off her pack and began assembling the glider. When it came to the runners she hesitated, trying to decide between the disadvantage of their weight and the protection they offered. She should have made a judgment on that before she even left the village. But she didn't have time to agonize; habit took over, and she snapped them into place. The ritual, completed, felt right now.

"Don't look back," she muttered. She'd lost track of how far away Joanna was, but if she turned for a last farewell it would only be harder for both of them. She put the cuttings in a pouch tied to her belt, strapped the glider onto her back, then ran toward the edge of the cliff as fast she could.

The wind was already behind her, drawn inward and upward by the geyser's flow. Her feet were barely touching the ground, and as she stepped off the cliff she ascended. Below her, she saw the fractured cone of uncrossable ice spread out in all its glittering, glorious irrelevance; she hooted down at it with delight and derision.

She looked up into a wall of white haze, and twisted the glider, sending it swerving right. This close, the geyser itself was too wide and diffuse to navigate by; she turned back to the ground, taking her cues from what she could still see of the cone through the ice-dust. She was rising faster than she'd expected; all the rehearsals in her head had played out far more slowly.

The cone disappeared, leaving her engulfed in whiteness everywhere she looked. She sent the glider left, and pictured it ascending in an ever-narrower helix. *Was she over the chasm?* It was impossible to tell. But if she waited any longer, and rose any higher, it would only increase the chance that anything she dropped would be blown aside on its way down.

She opened the pouch and watched the cuttings tumble away; as strong as the updraft was, they were dense and compact enough for their weight to overcome it. Ice was forming on her hands and face; she wanted to grimace, but she was afraid the fragments would cut her, even blind her.

All that mattered now was gaining speed. The whole flow of the geyser couldn't escape Tvíburi's gravity, or there would be no cone of fallen ice around it, and no soil added to any of the plateaus. But that didn't prove that every last particle the geyser emitted fell back to the ground. She just had to find the fastest portion, emerging from the very center of the chasm where friction with the walls had taken the least toll.

She turned the glider cautiously farther to the left, and felt an unmistakable tug as the air and ice-dust pushed harder against the panels. She settled into the flow, leaving her body almost weightless, then tried again, feeling her way into a faster current. There was nothing to see, nothing to guide her, but she found the right direction, over and over, until there was nowhere left to go.

The haze darkened; the sun had gone behind Tvíbura. The ocean below was being forced up into the chasm with as much pressure as it ever would be. Rosalind took a moment to inhale the sweet, rich air. On the ocean floor, the tiniest living creatures fed on an entirely different gas, created by nothing but water and hot minerals, and then exhaled this beautiful waste. If they hadn't existed, living out their strange lives in that hidden realm, nor would she.

The air grew thinner, and the haze dispersed. Rosalind watched the shadow of her home world racing across the ground. As far as she could tell, she was still ascending; the geyser had given her all it had to offer, and the only question now was whether that had been enough.

She thought about her mother, waiting for news of the first hint of Tvíburian crops. What would she think, when she learned of a very different discovery, closer to home? It might not be apparent who the messenger had been, but there were people who would recognize the smallest quirks in the style of any glider. Then again, that much of the structure didn't need to survive the landing; only the message itself had to arrive intact.

By the time the shadow sped away below her, the whole of Tvíburi had shrunk to the kind of disk she'd seen from the top of the tower. Inasmuch as she could discern her own motion at all, she was traveling west far faster than she was ascending; though she'd shared the speed of the rotating ground when she'd departed, this high up she would have needed a much greater eastward velocity to remain above the same spot. But fleeing to the west also meant fleeing Tvíbura. She might have crossed the line where it would still capture her; it might be slowing her escape at an imperceptible rate that would still be sufficient in the end. Or she might be destined to return to Tvíburi, far from the geyser, with nothing to do but start the long walk back to the village.

It was impossible to tell. She'd done her best, but her trajectory was out of her hands now. If she glided down onto the ice field, as smoothly as she'd first arrived, would she reproach herself for failing or would she rejoice that she'd been spared? Even with her brothers gone and her mind untainted, how could she want anything but to live?

Below her, the landscape kept changing, but the cycle of day and night seemed held in abeyance. She couldn't quite be outracing the sunset, but as time stretched on the disk of Tvíburi remained fully lit. Rosalind closed her eyes and pictured herself suspended in the sunlight forever, perfectly balanced between every hope she'd held for herself, and every hope she'd held for her people. Never falling, never coming down.

She had not done everything. The runners were the heaviest parts of the glider, and they could only serve their purpose if she failed. She should never have brought them with her.

She opened her eyes and reached down with both hands, feeling for the clips that held the runners to the frame. There were four clips on each side; she loosened them all, then worked the runners free.

Before she could talk herself out of it, she summoned all her strength and flung the runners away, sending them back down toward Tvíburi. She watched them retreating, trying to guess their speed, hoping that the small impetus she'd given the glider would make a difference.

She was naked now; wherever she landed it would be unsurvivable. She was every bit as dead as her brothers had been the moment she'd pushed in the knife. The horror of it only grew stronger, refusing to fade away. But what had she expected? To be at peace?

The glider had begun to rotate slowly; she'd thrown more powerfully with one arm than the other. Tvíbura came into view, still far from the zenith. She looked away, up at the underside of the glider as the sunlight fell on the panels. On each one, she'd written the same words, repeated half a dozen times. She read and re-read the message, clinging to it as the glider turned, until she saw dusk begin to creep across the limb of Tvíburi. Her home world hadn't let her escape; it was pulling her back to the east.

Rosalind reached up and gripped the handle bars, trying to stop herself from shaking so she could gather her thoughts and strengthen her resolve. She was not an inert piece of cargo; she still needed to do her best to keep the glider stable as she came into Tvíbura's thin atmosphere, and to steer as close as she could toward a place where the wreckage would be found. The panels would be shredded and scattered across the ice field, but it was up to her to ensure that someone would eventually stumble upon the fragments.

Although we can't grow the usual crops here, we are well-fed and safe. Do not be afraid to join us if you need to.

PART THREE

11 ~~~~~

PETRA lay harnessed to her sled, tense in the airless silence, stealing quick glances to either side to reassure herself that her mute companions hadn't taken their eyes away from their telescopes. The catapult would only be released if Kirsi and Rada tugged on the two levers at exactly the same time, in a unanimous vote that was meant to spare them all the consequences of an ill-timed attempt. But if any kind of error was possible, that included a lack of consensus that would prevent her from being launched at all. Waiting six days for the next opportunity would be unbearable.

She was spared the anti-climax: the sled shot forward and she was in the void. She turned and looked back toward the tower, elated. The rope trailing behind her lay in an almost perfect straight line, but the tug of the harness on her shoulders was as gentle as she could have wished. Ingrid and Lena were working the crank so smoothly that the rope they unwound was neither slack nor tense, neither holding her back nor looping dangerously ahead of her.

She quickly returned her gaze to the view ahead, determined not to be taken by surprise. However accurate the predictions of the libration had become, the team's ability to aim and calibrate the catapult remained the greatest source of uncertainty. The target might appear on her left or her right, outracing her or lagging behind. The only thing she was sure she could rule out was a head-on collision; they couldn't have achieved that themselves if they'd tried, and their errors were hardly going to conspire to make it happen.

A star blinked, then another, and another. Petra registered the events but couldn't yet extract any real sense of the occluding object's position and motion. Kirsi had spent more than a hundred nights staring through her telescope before she'd managed to record a sufficient number of occultations to be sure that the old tower was even standing; until then, for all anyone knew it might have crumbled to the ground. Petra had been in awe of her then, but now that she was actually approaching the thing and still couldn't interpret the fleeting evidence it offered for its existence, her admiration only increased. She would never have had that much patience.

Slowly, a dim gray thread emerged against the blackness, slightly to the left of the sled's forward bearing. From this distance, it seemed as remote and unreal as it did through the telescopes: more like a flaw in the lens than a solid object. But now there was no lens to bear the flaw, and when Petra closed each of her eyes in turn, the blemish remained.

As she watched, the thread thickened slightly, but it was also moving away to the left. She needed to change her trajectory, but acting too soon or too late would ruin the encounter. She estimated the angular speed of the target, then waited and did it again. Waited again. Estimated.

She pushed the lever on her own small catapult and sent a rock flying into the void to her right, at the same time loosening the brake on her rope spool. The sled responded with a brief, satisfying jolt, and the extra rope began playing out beside her. When the spool was half unwound, she tightened the brake again, and the right-angle bend she'd created began to deform. There was a huge amount of rope laid out along her original trajectory, and the rock she'd ejected hadn't possessed anything like the momentum needed to realign it all neatly behind her, but if she'd judged the timing correctly she'd have a good chance to make it to the tower before too much of the rope got the message that she'd changed direction.

The thread was a gray sliver now, slowly growing wider. Petra could discern a sharp boundary at one end—the "bottom," by her parochial reckoning—but when she followed it "up" toward Tvíbura, it just narrowed and dimmed until it had no visible effect on the stars behind it.

The tower passed by on her left, but they weren't done with each other yet. She looked back anxiously and watched the gray sliver cross over to her right. She'd overshot it twice now in different directions, but it was speeding up in the first direction, as it moved away from the closest point in the libration cycle, so it was only a matter of time before it overtook the rope she'd laid across its path—

The sled shuddered alarmingly, swung from side to side, then settled. When Petra looked back along the rope, the part she could see was pointing straight toward the tower. If everything had gone to plan, she was effectively tethered to her target now, with the tower's own acceleration keeping the rope pressed taut against it. And so long as nothing slipped or broke, she would keep on circling it, drawn ever closer as the rope wound her in.

She could feel a gentle tension in the rope, conveyed to her as a slight pressure from the harness. The stars wheeled slowly across the sky, but even when they'd come full circle it was hard to feel any sense of progress. It was only by the time she'd completed half a dozen orbits that she was able to convince herself that the cycles were growing shorter.

When Rada had suggested this method for the crossing, Petra's first instinct had been that conservation of angular momentum would impose an ever greater velocity on the traveler as she spiraled inward, which would either lead to the rope snapping from centrifugal tension, or deliver her to her destination with a speed she'd have no hope of countering or surviving. But that hunch had proved to be misplaced. The curious geometry of the spiral involute meant that the pull of the rope, while slowly changing the direction in which she was moving, would never increase her speed. The time it took her to loop around the tower was only shrinking because she was drawing closer—and rather than feeding her energy, the tower and Tvíbura were helpfully draining away her unwanted angular momentum.

She needed to be patient now, but vigilant too; with no real idea of her precise distance from the tower when it had snagged the rope, counting orbits wouldn't tell her much. All she knew for sure was the general character of motion along the involute: the distance from the center would change at an almost constant rate for a considerable time, only to start falling precipitously at the end.

The turning of the stars, with the same familiar constellations rolling into view over and over, risked lulling her into a state of dreamy torpor, but the slow revelation of the tower itself held her attention, however frustrating the pace. The walls of her own world's newer version were hardly perfect geometrical forms, but the old tower looked almost as if it had melted and flowed at times, or at least that its underlying vegetative skeleton had started to rebel and go wild. Petra did not expect anyone to have tended to it for a very long time, but she tried not to extrapolate too far from these undeniable signs of neglect. One forsaken structure was no fair measure of the state of a whole world.

When the rush finally came she was more than ready for it. The tower seemed to spiral in toward her, spinning as it approached, revealing ever richer details in its warped and pitted surface but moving too fast for her to dwell on any one feature. The extent of her motion "upward" toward Tvíbura had seemed quite small to her before, but now she could see that the helix she'd wound was pitched more steeply than she'd expected, and when she tried to find the point where the rope had first touched the wall, it was too distant to discern.

She'd already rewound her catapult and prepared it for its final task. Before the relentless spiraling left her disoriented, she ejected a second rock to oppose her motion, and suddenly the sky was all but still.

The sled had not been perfectly halted: it continued upward along the length of the tower, while also trying to pull away from it. Then the rope caught it and stopped it, briefly, before it rebounded inward and swung toward the wall. Petra was ready; she raised the baffle at the side of the sled, and when it struck the wall there was a thud she could feel through her bones, but no pain, and no apparent damage.

She waited for a while, prepared for the worst: for the helix to start unraveling. But gravity here was still negligible; it was not as if the coiled rope was having to support any real burden to stay in place. And in the tests on her own tower, the rope of tangler fibers had ended up not just wrapped around the ice, but bonded to it in places, the friction of the encounter having partly melted it.

Petra checked that her pack was secure, then untied her harness from the frame of the sled, leaving it joined only to the rope on a second spool. She released the brake on the spool—allowing it to turn almost freely, but with a governor to slow it if it spun too quickly—then clambered off the sled and floated beside the wall of the tower.

Now that she was no longer swayed by the notion of lying on her stomach on the sled, her sense of the vertical changed. The bulk of the tower, the part beyond the helix, was clearly below her. Tvíbura was the only way down.

She gave the sled a firm upward push, which had little effect on it but sent her body downward at the speed of a brisk walk. She watched the bumpy, mottled wall of the tower move past her.

She knew that the balcony couldn't be far, but it was a relief when she finally spotted it below her. She waited for it to come closer, then reached out and placed a gloved hand against the wall, careful not to apply pressure and push herself away. The friction wasn't much, but nor was her weight. She bent her knees as she struck the floor of the balcony; she bounced up again, but clawed at the wall and halted her ascent. The encounter pushed her away from the wall, but downward as well, and the balcony's outer, protective wall stopped her and sent her inward again. Petra forced herself to stay calm as she bounced from surface to surface; so long as she did nothing to gain energy, and nothing that sent her over the balcony, she'd have to come to a halt eventually.

When she was still, she lay on the floor for a while, grateful and amazed. The bridge might be far from complete, but the first strand was in place. The worlds would be joined, for anyone to cross between them at will. They had proved that it was possible.

∞

THE ICE WAS gone around the seals of the entrance from the balcony into the tower, which made it easy to get through the six doors, but meant at least one level of the tower would be devoid of air. Petra was unfazed; anything less would have left her resentful that she'd wasted so much time training in the void. The seals could be repaired eventually, the whole journey made infinitely easier, but the world would not begrudge her the satisfaction of being among the few prepared to go first.

Inside, the staircase looked almost familiar in design, but hallucinatory in detail. The Yggdrasil roots had had their way, retreating and advancing, laying down mounds of ice in one place, resorbing it in another. The stairs were still traversable, but the endless variation of bumps and pits rendered every footfall a surprise.

Petra descended as quickly as she could, taking advantage of the low gravity. She would be cautious once a fall might actually injure her, but if she dawdled now that would only make her more impatient later, and more tempted to take foolish risks. Apart from the breach at the entrance, the walls themselves appeared to have retained their integrity; for all the strange distortion and dimpling she encountered, there were no outright holes in the ice. As the sun dropped lower and came directly through the walls, it cast strange bright spots and twisted caustics over the central column. It was like the dappled light in one of the shallower tunnels through the tanglers.

She reached the bottom of the level just as night fell, and found the seals of the connecting chamber not just intact, but blocked by outgrowths of ice. She took the chisel from her pack, but then thought better of trying anything in the fading light. If she ruined the seals and lost all the air from another level, that would be unforgivable. So she spread her blanket on the floor beside the chamber, and slept.

∞

STANDING IN THE open air at the top of the final staircase, with the wind and dust of the ancestral world blowing in her face, Petra felt her brothers begin to stir.

The stairs she could see in front of her weren't any more malformed and bulbous than the thousands of helical ones she'd already negotiated, but the unbroken line from the landing to the still distant ground did induce a new kind of vertigo: if she slipped and fell, it wasn't clear how far she might descend before she came to a stop. The swollen ice on the side walls had spat out all the railings to which she might have hooked a safety rope; all she could do was keep her hands on the walls to steady herself, and take scrupulous care with where she placed her feet.

As she prepared to step off the landing, she felt her brothers rebel, all but paralyzing her with fear. She only had one more pessary left, and whatever progress her friends might have made on the rope bridge by the time she came back, she was fairly sure that her need to exercise unfettered judgment would be even greater then. "What would you have me do?" she muttered. "Stay here forever and starve to death?"

She still had food in her pack, of course. And whether her brothers were aware of that or not, she wasn't really arguing with them, so much as with a kind of conspiracy they'd formed with her own, more ancient instincts. Ancient Petra certainly knew about the food.

Modern Petra took off her pack, pulled out the sack of dried meat and tanglers, and tossed it down the stairs. It came to a halt before it vanished from sight, and it did not appear to have split open. She hadn't really intended the gesture as an experiment to test her own vulnerability, but the results were encouraging: even if she did fall, it might not be too terrible.

The conspiracy was appalled, but it was also hungry enough to be disinclined to walk away from food. Petra put her pack on and started making her way down, promising everyone that she'd start chewing on a tangler once she reached the sack—and hoping that it would seem easier and safer by then to continue down the stairs than it would to turn back.

∞

THE ICE FIELD around the base of the tower was desolate. If there had ever been tents or other buildings here, no trace of them remained.

Petra inhaled the thin, dusty air and contemplated the task ahead of her. The hemisphere visible through the telescopes contained no farms or grassland, and everything that wasn't ice resembled outcrops of bare rock, or pits of gray dust. But if Tvíburi had proved anything, it was that a food source didn't always look the way it was expected to look.

Evening was approaching, so she set up her tent in the partial shelter of one of the tripod legs. Whatever else had befallen Tvíbura, the ocean must still be thriving if the Yggdrasil that held the tower up hadn't withered and died. If only the people of the surface could have found a way to live down there in the sweltering darkness, sheltered from the vagaries of the sun and the geysers, floating through the molten ice.

In the morning, she set off east, guided by the sun but also looking up often at Tvíburi to impress the meaning of its features on her so she'd have no trouble reading them, day or night. The idea that she might somehow fail to find her way back to the tower did not remain unthinkable for long; by the end of her first day walking, it had vanished from sight, and while the maps in her pack were as detailed as she could make them from Tvíburi, down on the ground, for stride after stride, the only phrase her surroundings evoked was: *ice is ice.*

On the second day, it rained heavily, and she filled a bottle with ethane. When she squatted down to inspect the rivulets running over the ground, she saw fine dust pinned by surface tension to the top of the liquid, but no matter how closely she squinted at the surface she could not make out a single struggling insect.

On the third day, she reached a cluster of hills. She clambered over the rocks, in and out of shallow, sheltered valleys, but they concealed nothing she could recognize as living.

On the fifth day, with Tvíburi low in the sky, Petra came to a place that was known to have been farmland. The topography had kept the degraded soil from dispersing across the whole surrounding ice field, but the swirls of gray dust through which she strode did not remain still enough to make a home for any conceivable form of vegetation.

The fields were long gone, but where the center of the village must have stood, she found the remains of half a dozen buildings, with stone or wooden foundations set in pits hewn into the underlying ice. Petra knelt down between the ruins, covering her face against the dust. At least some of the people of this village had reached Tvíburi safely; that much was recorded in the archives. But what would she tell their descendants when she returned? That there had been no invisible salvation, no revolution in Tvíburan agriculture that could keep people fed as the soil blew away. No one had any right to be surprised by that, but she could not blame them for hoping otherwise.

When she set out on the seventh day, Tvíburi hung bisected on the horizon behind her. Petra felt a sense of panic at the prospect of losing sight of her own world; once it vanished, she might find herself wandering endlessly beneath an empty sky. But she stared down her fears and kept walking. Every place where she'd set foot until now had been scrutinized for generations, and all that anyone had seen through their telescopes had been farm after farm dying. But half the world had remained hidden, and from the day the last migrants had alighted on the Tvíburian ice, no more news of its fate had been forthcoming. Many people had made the Great Walk on Tvíburi—and at least in the past, on Tvíbura too. If she wanted to return with a final answer on the fate of this world, the only way was to revive that tradition.

12 ~~~~~~

PETRA didn't expect the old maps of the far side to tell her much; when she'd compared migration-era maps of the visible hemisphere with current, telescopic versions, four out of every five villages had vanished entirely. But with nothing else to guide her, she sought out the places where people had once lived.

Sometimes it was difficult to know if she'd reached the right site and found nothing, or simply failed to pin down the correct location. Unlike farmland and grassland, hills and mountains didn't blow away in the wind, but it was rare that they could serve as reliable signposts.

By her thirteenth day on Tvíbura, all her food had run out. She'd been expecting that, and as an abstract idea it didn't worry her; all her training told her she could keep up her strength and complete the Great Walk in thirty days, at which point Rada would be waiting for her at the base of the tower with fresh supplies. But starving herself by choice, as an exercise, within half a day's walk of her own village back home, was not the same as marching empty-handed over an endless expanse of barren ice on the most distant part of a world that for all she knew was entirely lifeless.

On the morning of the fourteenth day, as Petra was disassembling her tent, she noticed a strange bulge on the horizon. It looked like a small mountain range, except that it was the color of ice, not rock. To explore it, she would need to detour to the north, and it seemed to correspond to nothing on her map. But then, either she was lost and this landmark would help to set her straight, or it was something genuinely new that merited investigation.

By mid-afternoon, the formation had come into clearer view, but that only made it less comprehensible. The "mountains" really were made of ice—or at least covered in it—but their shape was neither that of any rocky structure Petra had ever seen, or anything the elements had been known to carve out of the ice field. For a long time, she simply doubted that she was perceiving their geometry correctly; with a single viewpoint, changing so slowly, she lacked the cues to verify the full, three-dimensional forms that her mind kept proposing, then rejecting, then stubbornly returning to. But before night fell and she was left with nothing but starlight, she'd almost convinced herself: someone had tried to grow half a dozen separate Yggdrasil towers in the ice, all side-by-side. And then either by mishap, or by very strange design, they had all ceased growing vertically, and stretched out instead in more or less the same horizontal direction.

Dawn revealed nothing that made Petra change her mind, apart from one minor refinement: while five of the towers had remained upright, supporting the weight of their eccentric offshoots, the second from the left had toppled over in the direction of the overhang, but then rather than falling sideways as well it had come to a halt leaning against its neighbor.

She packed up her tent and strode toward the deformed towers as fast as she could. The wind was blowing strongly against her, but she had no intention of passing another night without resolving the mystery.

The only reason she could think of to grow an ice tower on the side of the world facing away from Tvíburi was in the hope of creating a geyser. But the stories all declared that Freya had proved such efforts futile—and while Petra could understand people doubting that those old fairground experiments had been conclusive, seeing the full-scale version stretching up into the sky without sinking its own foundations had surely been a great deal more persuasive.

Something touched her face, and she slapped at it instinctively. When she examined her palm, there was a soft, dark smear: the body of an insect.

Petra broke into a run, but her destination was too far away for a single burst of optimism to carry her there, so she slowed to a walk and conserved her strength. Sprinting to the point of collapse only to find a tiny patch of grassland clinging on behind the towers would not be worth it.

∞

THE SUN WAS setting as she approached the feet of the towers. To Petra's eye, they looked infinitely more misshapen and neglected than the one she'd descended, but if no one had ever been meant to climb them, different standards applied.

To the west, the sun was framed by the ramshackle arch of the fallen tower. Petra headed for the gap between the central pair, anxious as she passed below one of the overhangs, as if it might choose this very moment to tear itself free and crash to the ground. Staring up at the huge, horizontal column of ice, she thought of the tree branches she'd seen in the picture books passed down through her family. But no tree had ever stopped and sprouted a single branch of the same girth as its trunk.

She'd swatted a few more insects along the way, but she had to be ready to find herself among ruins as grim as any of the dead villages she'd passed through. When she reached the base of the tower, twilight had already descended, and whatever lay ahead was lost in the gloom. She stopped and prepared to set up camp.

"Who goes there?" a voice demanded.

Petra froze, unable to reply, though the tone had been more curious than threatening.

"Who is it?" The woman sounded annoyed now, rather than aggressive, as if she'd decided that a friend was playing a joke on her.

"My name's Petra," Petra called back into the darkness.

"Who?"

"Petra. Can I ask your name?"

A figure strode out of the shadows. "I'm Ebba," the woman replied irritably, as if that ought to have been obvious. "Why don't I know you? Which village are you from?"

Petra said, "I've come from far away."

Ebba snorted. "Far away? Nothing's far away."

"I've come from Tvíburi," Petra explained.

She couldn't really see Ebba's face, but the woman seemed to be scrutinizing her strange, coarse clothing. "What kind of nonsense is that? Are you telling me you flew here?"

"No. We finished our tower, and joined it with yours. There was some rope involved, but no untethered flight." Petra was starting to wonder if she was dreaming, or had simply lost her mind. "We were afraid that everyone here might be dead."

Ebba walked right up to her and grasped her shoulders, as if to check that she was awake herself, and that Petra was not her own hallucination.

She said, "We were afraid you were all dead, too. We thought the first travelers must have starved to death, along with every crazy woman who followed them on the basis of nothing but a scrawl on a fragment of a broken glider."

Petra started sobbing. Ebba embraced her clumsily, hushing her. "Well, neither world is dead, so there's only good news."

"But what do you eat?"

"The usual kind of food."

"Grown how? How do you still have soil?"

Ebba released her. "You didn't see it, as you were approaching?"

"See what?"

"You must have been too far away." Ebba caught herself. "And you must be very tired and hungry."

Petra followed her through the darkness. She could smell the soil now, and some complicated scent carried on the breeze that she could only assume was a melange of old-world vegetation: grass, crops, trees. Ebba led her into a house, to a lamplit room, where two other women were preparing food.

The three of them conversed in whispers, then Ebba introduced her friends as Laila and Tone.

"You came down through the old tower?" Laila asked, as if that were the most surprising aspect of Petra's journey.

"Yes."

"I went there once. I started walking up the stairs to see if I could get a nice view, but then I changed my mind and came down."

Petra said, "Quite right. The stairs have lost their shape and they're very slippery."

She sat at the table and ate, in a daze, confused by the peculiar flavors and textures but not repelled; some part of her body welcomed every mouthful, more than it had ever welcomed her chewing on a tangler. She answered the women's questions as best she could, though some words in their dialect were utterly opaque to her. When she tried to think of sensible questions of her own, her mind shrank away from the task. After a while, her eyelids became heavy, then Ebba led her to another room and gestured to the blanket on the floor.

WHEN PETRA WOKE, she could tell from the light that it was long after dawn. For a moment she felt ashamed, as if she'd failed to attend in a timely manner to some important duty, and betrayed herself to her hosts as lazy and ungrateful. But as her mind cleared, she decided that she had no reason to reproach herself. She'd come a long way; she could be forgiven for sleeping till mid-morning.

When she left the room where she'd spent the night, she found the rest of the house empty, so she walked outside, squinting at the brightness. Stretched out in front of her was a row of similar houses; beyond them, an expanse of green fields full of low, leafy plants, interspersed with what she took to be orchards.

Past the fields, there were more villages, and more fields, and on it went, until behind the most distant fields there was a row of ice towers. At first Petra thought they were the ones she'd seen as she'd arrived, but that made no sense; she hadn't walked that far. As she turned her gaze to take in the whole impossible, idyllic scene, she realized that there was a ring of towers, encircling all of the agricultural land. Maybe twenty or thirty in total.

There were women walking along paths between the fields, and when Petra caught their gaze they raised their hands in greeting. No one came scowling to inquire about her origins; they must have been told already. Petra found a bench and sat, taking in the morning sun.

Ebba approached, carrying a basket full of something that looked disturbingly like tangler nodules, but were probably actually edible. "How did you sleep?" she asked Petra.

"Deeper than I've ever slept before." Petra wanted to thank her for her hospitality, but then thought better of it; it might be insulting to suggest that she would ever have treated a stranger otherwise. "Can I ask you something?"

Ebba said, "Of course."

"Where does all the soil come from?"

Ebba turned and looked out across the fields. "If you can be patient for a moment longer, you'll see for yourself."

Petra didn't mind waiting. Ebba joined her on the bench.

"You came all this way thinking that we might be clinging to life, desperate to join the migration?"

Petra said, "Can you blame us? Nothing we could see through the telescopes looked good."

"We *were* desperate," Ebba conceded. "In my grand-mother's time, a lot of people starved. This place is beautiful, but it took generations of work to complete, and it can only feed so many of us."

"Your grandmother worked on the towers?"

"Yes."

Petra heard a faint hissing sound, somewhere in the dis-tance. She turned toward it, and saw a slender column of white ascending from the middle of the fields. Compared to the geysers on her own world, it was ridiculously modest, as if the crack in the ice through which it flowed might be barely a hand's breadth wide. But then, if it ran slowly and never rose high, whatever soil it delivered would not be scattered uselessly across the distant ice fields. It would all rain down upon the farms.

"The towers are so small," she said.

"Yes," Ebba agreed. "But they're unbalanced in a way that puts the ice under stress—and more so at a distance than directly beneath them, so the effects of several towers can be combined. We found a spot where the ice was weak already, where an old geyser had once flowed. Freya showed that you can't punch a hole through a slab of flawless ice just by piling up weight on top of it. But where there was a crack before, there's a chance. We built rings of towers like this in seventeen different places. This is the only one that worked."

Petra piled up all those towers, failed and fruitful, in her mind's eye; nothing had come easily to anyone. She said, "Everyone will have the chance to walk on the two worlds now. We can travel, we can trade, we can bring the most distant cousins together. The hard times are over."

The white column rose higher, summoned by the sun. Petra closed her eyes. She'd stay here and rest for a few more days, meet Rada to share the good news, then climb back to the void she loved, and join the others working on the bridge between the worlds, strand by strand, until it was complete.